Dear Reader,

I'd always be[en] ... [spor]t
of figure skating ... [seem]ed
magical to me. Add the discipline and hard work
needed to reach perfection and it was enough to
keep me enthralled.

And the Olympics? The excitement of competition, the once in a lifetime chance to take the gold?
What could I do? I had to write a story centered
around the Olympics and a skater who had worked
all her life to win that medal. Yes, this is a passionate and romantic story, and I loved creating Dany
Alexander and Anthony Malik. But I hope that
you'll also be able to glimpse a little of the passion
and beauty of the sport itself. If that happens, then
I've done my job.

Enjoy!

Iris Johansen

Iris Johansen

Books by Iris Johansen

IRIS JOHANSEN

White Satin

BANTAM BOOKS
NEW YORK

2010 Bantam Books Mass Market Edition

Copyright © 1985 by Iris Johansen

Published in the United States by Bantam Books,
an imprint of The Random House Publishing Group,
a division of Random House, Inc., New York.

BANTAM BOOKS and the rooster colophon are
registered trademarks of Random House, Inc.

Originally published in mass market in the United States by
Bantam Loveswept, an imprint of The Random House Publishing
Group, a division of Random House, Inc., in 1990.

ISBN 978-0-553-59370-9

Cover design: Eileen Carey
Cover image: © David Roth/Getty Images

Printed in the United States of America

www.bantamdell.com

9 8 7 6 5 4 3 2 1

White Satin

Chapter 1

Oh, please, let it be 5.7, Dany prayed silently, her hands clenching the stems of the roses she was holding. Hardly anyone ever got a perfect score— a 6.0—but she could come close. Only a few minutes earlier she'd scooped the roses up from the ice and waved them at the audience with a bright smile of appreciation as she glided around the rink. Anthony had taught her to do that as he'd taught her everything else. "A crowd-pleaser," he'd said with that cynical little smile. "It's always your business to please your audience, Dany."

But it wasn't the audience she had to worry about today; it was the judges. She'd always had an empathy with the audience. She could feel their warmth and admiration reach out to enfold her every time she skated out onto the ice to do a routine. They were always with her all the way, and she was passionately grateful for that support. She'd needed it today when she'd found out Anthony wasn't going to be there for the finals.

Shifting the flowers, she rubbed her palms nervously on the sheer silver chiffon of her skating costume, her gaze fixed on the judges across the sports arena from her. "Why can't they hurry?" she whispered.

"The scores should be coming up any minute, sugar," Beau Lantry said soothingly, his own face tense. "That third judge has been handing in her scores late all evening." His hand fell bracingly on her shoulder. "It's not a life-or-death decision, you know." His lazy southern drawl flowed like molasses over her taut nerves. "One competition isn't going to break you, Dany."

"Tell that to Anthony," Dany said dryly. She drew a deep, steadying breath. "He doesn't understand failure. Particularly in an important competition like the United States Championships."

"True." Beau's lips twisted ironically. "Still, he probably won't be angry at you, only at me. I'm your coach, and all blame falls on my humble head. I've never heard him raise his voice to you in all the years I've been working for him."

"He's never had to." All he had to do was gaze at her in silence with silver-green eyes that could be as glacier-cold as a Norwegian ice floe. Then he could proceed to tear her entire routine apart with an incisive brilliance that left her feeling as miserably unsure of herself as she'd felt as a child. No, more unsure. He'd been kinder to her then. Not warmer, but certainly more tolerant than the relentless mentor he'd become since she'd won the Juniors.

The scores for technical merit flashed on the board and she heard a disappointed groan from the crowd. She tabulated frantically and bit her lip. Not high enough to carry her over the top.

"Don't worry," Beau said. "You'll make it up in artistic impression. You always do."

"Maybe," she murmured under her breath.

Then the second set of scores began to light up

the board one after another. They were even lower than the first set. The composite score couldn't possibly be over a 5.6, Dany thought. She needed a 5.7. Second place. She hadn't won the championship. Oh, Lord, what was Anthony going to say?

Beau suddenly whirled her around to face him so that her back was to the arena. He had a determined smile fixed on his lean, handsome face, and his hazel eyes were warm with sympathy. "Keep facing me for a while, honey," he said easily. "You'll be all right in a minute, but you know how those TV cameras love to zoom in on the losers. You don't want them to see how upset you are."

"No, I don't want them to see that," she said dully. Anthony had taught her to keep a bright, smiling mask in place no matter what happened. He'd be more upset than ever if she fell apart in public. She knew a sudden flare of anger that speared through the anxiety and disappointment she was feeling. If he wanted her to be so damn perfect, why wasn't he here to help her? Dany asked herself. Why wasn't he here? She composed her features into a bland mask and returned

Beau's smile with a bright, meaningless one of her own. "I'm okay now," she said quietly. "Thanks for shielding me." She turned around to face the cameras, her expression serene as she waited to skate out to the rostrum to receive her medal and congratulate Margie on winning first place. Oh, Lord, why did it have to happen now? She'd been winning everything in sight all year, and now, just a month before the Olympics, she had to lose to Margie Brandon. She'd be going into the Olympics in Calgary with everyone in the sports world wondering if she was slipping.

"They're ready for you," Beau said softly, giving her a gentle nudge toward the ice. "Just a little longer and you can go to your dressing room and shut them all out. There's a TV sports commentator waiting in the corridor, but I'll bail you out after a few minutes."

"Thanks, Beau. I know you will." This time her smile was warm with affection. She didn't know what she'd do without Beau's kindness in moments like this. She glided out on the ice toward the rostrum. Her slight, fragile body moved with the liquid grace that had made her a champion; her head, crowned with silky auburn hair, was held high with indomitable pride.

Twenty minutes later, as she tried to fend off the questions of the sports commentator in the hall outside her dressing room, she wasn't quite so confident of Beau's ability to extricate her. She'd found most sports reporters to be sympathetic, but Jay Monteith was as persistent and feral as a weasel. All of Beau's attempts to whisk her out of his clutches had been futile.

"You've been the United States champion for the past two years, Miss Alexander," Monteith said. "It must be very upsetting to be toppled from your throne this close to the Olympics. Will this change your training plans?" He thrust the microphone at her as if it were a weapon.

"Naturally I'm not happy about it," Dany said, keeping her voice carefully expressionless. "But it really won't affect my training plans. I was going to work extremely hard this month anyway."

"How does Anthony Malik feel about your defeat?" Monteith asked, his dark eyes narrowed on her face to catch any flickering change of expression. "I noticed he's not here today. Has he been told that the queen has been deposed?"

"I have no idea," she said coolly. What a thoroughly unpleasant little man, Dany thought. He must have studied at the Howard Cosell school of journalism. "I haven't heard from Mr. Malik yet, so I would assume he hasn't heard. However, I'm sure my guardian will be very supportive as usual."

"*Supportive* being the key word," Monteith said silkily. "I understand Malik has spent over two hundred thousand dollars on you since you were a small child, training and promoting you into your present position. I wouldn't think he'd be any too pleased at having a loser on his hands at this stage of the game. At your age he'd won every figure-skating medal that had been invented, including the Olympic gold. Are you finding that kind of reputation hard to live up to?"

"No, why should I?" she asked crisply. "I compete against myself when I'm on the ice, not against anyone else. Nor do I compete to be compared to others. Anthony Malik is a legend in figure skating. There was never anyone like him before he appeared on the scene and there's never been anyone to compare with him since. That doesn't mean I can't carve my own niche in the sport."

Monteith persisted. "What kept Malik away from the competition?"

Why hadn't Anthony been here, dammit? Didn't he know how she needed him? "He's been a very busy man since he inherited complete control of the Dynathe Corporation," she said haltingly. "I'm sure he would have been here if he could."

"Are you going to be——"

"You'll have to excuse Miss Alexander," Beau drawled, opening her dressing room door and practically pushing her inside. "She's had a very exhausting day and has a plane to catch." He cast a glance at the slender gold watch on his wrist. "In just two hours." He backed into the room, still smiling genially. "I knew you boys would understand." The door closed with gentle firmness.

Marta Paulsen bustled forward, her plump, square body almost militant. "Why didn't you get

her away from them sooner?" she asked Beau
tartly as she pushed Dany down into a chair and
knelt to unlace her skates. "I was about to come
out and yank her in myself. Who did that squirt
Monteith think he was? If Anthony had been here,
he wouldn't have gotten away with that crap."
She glanced up at Dany as her strong broad hands
deftly dispensed with the laces. "You were robbed.
That Brandon girl looked like a cow on the ice."

Dany shook her head. "She was good. She's im-
proved a lot since last year." She reached down to
pat Marta's frizzy blond head, affectionately.
"You always say I've been robbed. You know very
well I was off today." She looked deliberately at
Beau, who'd dropped into the straight chair
across the room. "And so do you, Beau."

Beau stretched his tweed clad legs lazily before
him. "I've seen you in better form," he admitted.
"You seemed a bit mechanical toward the end.
Your technique was pretty good though."

"Mechanical!" Marta's voice was indignant.
"There's never been anything mechanical about
Dany's skating."

9

"Until today," Dany said wearily. "Let's face it, my technique and artistry were both below par."

"Well, that Brandon cow sure wasn't any Pavlova," Marta grumbled, her blue eyes soft with sympathy. She slipped the second skate off Dany's foot and massaged the instep with strong, skilled hands. "You're tied up in knots. Strip down and let me loosen you up a little before you shower."

Dany leaned back in the chair and closed her eyes. That sounded perfectly wonderful. As a masseuse Marta was superb. Her fingers were absolute magic on taut, rigid muscles. She had a motherly figure and had an enormous amount of strength in her arms and shoulders. "In a minute. Just let me relax for a while."

"Sorry, Dany, you don't have the time," Beau said. "Not for the massage, nor to relax either. The plane that leaves in two hours is the last one from Denver to Salt Lake City today. Anthony will want you to be checked in at that Inn at Parke City tonight and to get plenty of rest."

She opened her eyes. "Then, of course, we'll do as our lord and master decrees," she said, her lips twisting in a bittersweet smile. "We wouldn't want to offend the great man by changing his plans for our convenience."

Beau straightened slowly and ran his hand absently through his modishly cut bronze hair. "No, we wouldn't." His gold-flecked hazel eyes were grave. "We all owe Anthony a hell of a lot. He doesn't ask a great deal in exchange for what he gives."

"Only obedience and service twenty-four hours a day, three hundred and sixty-five days a year," Dany said tartly. Why was she talking like this? She owed Anthony everything and she knew it. It was as if something hurtful were goading her to say the words. Beau and Marta were both gazing at her in surprise, and their expressions only served to aggravate the uncharacteristic defiance she was feeling. "Why are you looking at me like that? Have I committed lèse-majesté against our omnipotent leader? Why is everyone so afraid of him, for heaven's sake?"

"I'm not afraid of Anthony." Beau's gaze was thoughtful on her face. "And I don't think Marta is either." His slow drawl held a trace of speculation. "But I think you are. I never realized that before. Why, Dany? He's always been exceptionally generous with you."

Two hundred thousand dollars, Dany mused, everything money and power could buy, his time and energy for the last twelve years. Exceptionally generous. Everything except love and affection. But then Anthony didn't give those particular gifts to anyone. She *was* a little afraid of him, she realized with a sense of shock, and more bitter with him for those gifts he'd withheld than she'd believed possible. "Why should I be afraid?" she asked, evading Beau's keen hazel eyes. "As you say, he's been very kind to me." She shook her head unhappily. "Oh, I don't know. I'm all confused. I think losing the title may have shaken me up more than I realized. Forget I said anything."

"Sure." Beau rose lithely to his feet. "None of us are any too happy about it, sugar. But like I said, it's not as if it were the Olympics. Put it behind you and learn from it." The phone on the dressing table rang shrilly, and he reached for the receiver. "I'll get it. You'd better get moving if we're going to get to the airport on time." He spoke into the phone. "Lantry." The casualness in his voice abruptly vanished. "Hello, Anthony."

Dany stiffened, her dark eyes flying to Beau's face and trying to read his expression.

"Yes, she's right here. Shall I put her on?" Evidently he was answered in the negative, for he shook his head when Dany made a movement to get up and come to the phone. "Well, she's not jumping for joy. She knows she blew it. We'll probably have to tie her up to keep her from working from sunrise to sunset at Parke City to iron out the problems." He listened for a long time, surprise flickering over his face. "You're sure? We'll have to deep-six all the plans we've made for the next month." There was a long silence on Beau's part, and Dany could almost hear the vibrant incisiveness of Anthony's voice. "Okay. I'll have her there by tomorrow afternoon at the latest." Beau replaced the receiver and turned to Dany. "He saw the competition on television." He grimaced. "He wasn't at all pleased. He said to scrap the plans for Parke City and come back to Briarcliff pronto. He wants us to get to New York tomorrow, and he'll send Pete Drissell with the car to meet us at La Guardia and drive us on to Connecticut."

"Briarcliff," Dany whispered. She hadn't been to Briarcliff for six years. She'd been fourteen then and had just won the Juniors. The year everything had changed. The year Anthony had changed. Since that time her training had all been conducted at various resorts around the country. Anthony had given the excuse that she needed to become accustomed to different rinks for competition purposes, and to gain more poise and independence, but she'd known that wasn't the reason she had been evicted from the only home she'd ever known. She'd gotten in his way. He'd become tired of having her underfoot, and after that ghastly afternoon in February he couldn't get rid of her fast enough. "He really wants us to come home?"

Beau nodded. "That's what he says. But don't expect a rip-roaring welcome. He sounded pretty grim."

Dany didn't care how he sounded. She was going home to Briarcliff. Home to Anthony.

* * *

"I've never seen you this excited before," Beau said, his gaze on her tense face curious.

Their chauffeured limousine paused at the electronically controlled gates to the estate. Pete Drissell pressed a button on the dashboard to activate the release on the lock of the gates, and they slid open.

"You're all lit up inside," Beau murmured.

"I haven't been home since I was fourteen," Dany said, peering eagerly out the window past Marta's plump profile. She wished now she'd insisted on sitting by the window. "This gate and stone wall are new since I was here last."

"Is it? It's always been here since I've been coming to Briarcliff." Beau shrugged. "Of course, I've only dropped by to give reports on your progress when Anthony wasn't at the apartment in New York. I suppose he decided that the estate needed more protection and privacy than it had when you were here."

"I liked it better without it." It was just like Anthony to build walls to shut the world out, Dany thought, her gaze fixed on the rambling Tudor-style brick house at the top of the hill. The two-story mansion was built of mellow pink brick, and the lead-glass windows and graceful fanlight over the front door gave it an air of warm, open invitation. Why had Anthony bought it when it was sold after her parents were killed in that boating accident? It wasn't his type of home at all. Even as a child she'd been aware of that. Anthony was as uneasy in cozy domestic surroundings as an unfettered panther would be.

"You lived here all your life until you were fourteen?" Beau asked, and immediately recalled the answer to his question. "Of course. Anthony was a friend of your parents, wasn't he?" His forehead knotted thoughtfully. "He became your guardian when you were eight, and they'd been killed in that accident. He must have been very close to them to assume the responsibilities of a kid so willingly. Anthony isn't what you'd call the fatherly type."

"I guess so," Dany admitted. That was, she knew, a distinct understatement. "I remember him being around the estate occasionally when I was five or six." But he hadn't really been close to her carefree, jet-setter parents. Beneath that glittery veil of charm he drew about himself on occasion, Dany had been aware of a dislike that was close to animosity whenever the four of them were together. She'd sensed it with a child's unwavering instinct and been surprised that her parents hadn't felt it. She shouldn't have been, she supposed. Her parents hadn't been especially sensitive to anything that didn't affect their own comfort and pleasure.

But it seemed totally absurd. Anthony couldn't possibly have had any other reason than affection and a sense of obligation to her parents when he'd sued for guardianship of her. Dany shook her head in bewildered frustration as the limousine pulled smoothly to a halt before the front entrance. Why did she even try to fathom Anthony's motivation for anything? He was a law unto himself, an enigma she hadn't been able to solve for the past twelve years.

Pete Drissell, the chauffeur who was opening the passenger door and helping Marta and her from the limousine, was a quietly courteous young man and as unfamiliar to her as the black-jacketed, gray-haired servant who opened the front door.

"Miss Alexander? I'm Paul Jens. Mr. Malik is waiting for you in the library." His voice was meticulously polite. "He asked me to send you there immediately upon your arrival. I'll have one of the maids take up your luggage to the room I understand you occupied previously. I'll take Mr. Lantry and Miss Paulsen to their rooms now if they'll follow me." The polite query was really a command, and Beau gave Dany a resigned shrug as he allowed Marta and her to precede him into the spacious oak parquet–tiled foyer.

"Looks as though you're destined to beard the lion in his den alone, sugar," he said as he started to follow Paul Jens up the wide, curving stairway. "I'll see you at dinner."

"Don't let him keep you too long," Marta warned. "You need a nap. You didn't sleep very much on that jet. You can't afford to exhaust yourself unnecessarily with the kind of schedule you've got."

"I'll give Anthony your instructions," Dany

said wryly as she slipped off her beige cashmere polo coat and draped it over her arm. "For all the good it will do me." Evidently Anthony wasn't even going to give her an opportunity to settle in and renew her acquaintance with Briarcliff before he demanded an explanation for yesterday's debacle.

She dropped her coat on the long cushioned bench against the wall and walked quickly down the corridor to the library. She paused for a moment before an oval mirror framed in glowing mahogany to tidy her auburn hair into its usual neat bun on top of her head. *Heavens*, she thought, *I look terrible*. Her thin, delicate face was even more fragile-appearing than usual, and her dark eyes with their frame of extravagantly long lashes had mauve shadows beneath them. Not exactly a facade to inspire confidence when she was about to face a powerhouse like Anthony. Well, even at her best she'd never been able to confront him with the same poise with which she handled the public and the media.

She drew a deep breath as she paused outside the richly paneled oak door of the library. How stupid to have this crazy fluttering in the pit of her stomach. He wasn't going to eat her, for heaven's sake. She raised her hand and knocked firmly on the door.

"Come in."

He was sitting in a huge leather chair pushed back from the mahogany desk that was the central focus of the room. As usual, her first impression of him was one of dynamic strength and overpowering magnetism.

She could see all of him. He was dressed casually in jeans and a crew-neck sweater in a cream color that made the bronze of his skin and the satin darkness of his hair gleam with added vibrancy in contrast. There wasn't an ounce of fat on the lean, graceful body, and the sinewy power of his shoulders and the muscular strength of his thighs only accented his supple slenderness.

There was a swift flicker of emotion in the silver-green of his eyes as he saw her standing waiting in the doorway, but it was gone in an instant. He gestured to the deep russet leather chair next to the desk. "Sit down, Dany. I've been waiting for you." He pushed aside the pile of documents he'd been working on. He appraised her coolly, from the hip-length, cowl-neck caramel-colored sweater and matching slacks to the darker brown short suede boots. "You've lost weight again. I thought you had when I saw you on television yesterday. Beau says you're overdoing the practice and not eating enough."

"Evidently he's wrong—about the practice at least," she said flippantly as she closed the door and strolled over to the chair he'd indicated. "Judging by the results of the competition yesterday, I need all the practice I can get." She dropped into the chair and raised her brows inquiringly. "I gather that's why I'm here." She glanced down at the kilim carpet that ran almost the length of the library. "Well, if I'm to be called on the carpet, this is a very attractive one on which to abase myself. I don't recognize it. It's new, isn't it?" She looked up at him, a hint of challenge in her expression. "There are quite a few changes since I left. A new wall and gate, different servants, new furniture."

He leaned back in the chair, one knee lifting to rest against the edge of the desk. His eyes were narrowed thoughtfully on her face. "I like to leave my own stamp on my surroundings," he said slowly. "I've never been satisfied to accept someone else's choices or hand-me-downs"—a little smile tugged at his lips—"even if those hand-me-downs happen to be antiques." The smile faded. "But as it happens, I did want to talk to you."

"I gathered that from the way you pulled us halfway across the country with the speed of light," she said dryly. She moistened her lips nervously and looked away from him to a point over his shoulder. There was such power in his dark, impassive face. When she was away from him, she always thought her imagination was playing tricks and exaggerating his forcefulness. There was nothing conventionally handsome about him. His cheekbones were too high and broad, his lips a touch too sensual, and his chin too firm for classical good looks. It made no sense at all that when combined, those features formed a countenance with a totally riveting fascination about it. Or was his most salient characteristic that air he always exuded of something leashed and waiting beneath the cool stillness? That charged stillness was even more obvious than usual today, Dany thought uneasily. "Look, why don't I just bring it out in the open? I blew the competition. I don't know what was wrong, but I'll find out and work myself to a frazzle to correct it." She drew a deep breath and forced herself to look into those cool green eyes. They caught and held her, and she had a panicky feeling of something ebbing away deep inside her. "I won't let you down, Anthony. I'll be ready for Calgary."

"You're damn right you will be," he said, a touch of grimness in his voice. "I'm going to see to that personally. There wasn't any reason for you to not win yesterday. You're a hell of a lot better technically and artistically than Margie Brandon. You were skating like a puppet on a string. You had more fire when you won the Juniors six years ago."

"I said I'd work on it," she answered defensively. "You don't have to waste your time overseeing my training yourself. I know how busy you are."

"So you told that ass of a sports commentator yesterday," he said, a dark frown creasing his forehead. "I'll be the one to judge how busy I am, Dany."

"Whatever you say," she said with an effort at lightness. "You've become such a high-powered tycoon lately that I just thought it would be too much bother." She paused. "You haven't coached me personally since you hired Beau and Marta and sent me away from Briarcliff."

"Do you think I'm not capable of the job?" he asked, an amused smile on his lips. "I believe I still have sufficient expertise to give you what you need."

"No, I didn't mean . . ." She stammered to a halt, cursing his effect on her. She was always such a quivering bundle of nerves around Anthony. "You know I meant no such thing," she said with careful composure. "I've been told you're still considered by most authorities to be the greatest figure skater who ever lived. When you retired from the Ice Revue to take over the Dynathe Corporation, you threw the whole sports world into shock."

"Then you'll accept my humble tutelage?" There

was a glimmer in his eyes that might have been laughter.

"When have I ever had a choice?" she asked lightly. "You know you'll do exactly as you please both with me and my career, just as you've always done."

"Not always." His voice had deepened, and there was a sudden electric tenseness waiting beyond the stillness. "But I intend to do just that from now on. It's only fair to warn you, Dany. I find I'm growing very impatient of late."

"For the gold?" she asked, puzzled. "I told you I'd work myself to a frazzle. I realize it's going to be more your medal than mine after all you've done for me. You'll have your gold, Anthony."

"No!" The word was spoken with such explosiveness, it startled her. "I have my own gold medal. I don't want or need yours. When you win at Calgary, it's got to be the crown of *your* achievements, *your* work. It's got to be *your* victory, not mine or Beau's."

"Of course. I know that," she faltered. Why was he so intense about it? His eyes were almost blazing. "I just meant that I realize how much I owe you—"

"For God's sake, shut up!" Then, as her eyes widened in surprise, he drew a deep breath, and the cool mask was once more in place. "You don't know what you're talking about."

She felt a deep, throbbing hurt. "I'm not a child anymore, you know. I'd appreciate it if you wouldn't speak to me like that."

"I know you're not a child. Sometimes I think you never were, that you were born old." His lips twisted. "Some of us are, you know." He picked up the pen he'd tossed down as she'd entered and toyed with it absently. "That's why it's been so damn difficult for me at times. You may possess the inner maturity, but you don't have the experience that would temper and refine it."

"Difficult?"

"Never mind." His fingers tightened spasmodically on the pen before he slowly released it. "After Calgary."

"All right." Her eyes were dark with bewilderment. She'd never seen Anthony this volatile before. It made her more uneasy than ever. She started to rise. "If that's all, I think I'll—"

"That's not all," he said crisply. "Sit down, Dany. Your performance was a disaster yesterday, but that's not why I brought you back from Denver."

"It isn't?"

He reached into the top desk drawer and drew out a folded newspaper. "This is why you're here." His lips were tight and his eyes glacier-cold as he handed her the paper. "You look exceptionally affectionate. How long has this been going on?"

She'd seen the picture the night before last in *The Denver Post,* but she hadn't known it had been picked up by the wire services. "He's only got his arm around me," she said quickly, feeling the color surge to her cheeks. How ridiculous to feel guilty over something so innocent, she thought. "It's not as if we were locked in a torrid embrace or anything. You can't find anything objectionable in publicity like that."

"Can't I?" he drawled. He reached across the desk and plucked the paper from her hand, then slowly and systematically wadded it into a ball and threw it into the wastebasket. "I do find it objectionable. Very objectionable. You haven't answered me. How long has this affair been going on?"

"It's not an affair," she said, stung. "I've only been out to dinner with Jack Kowalt a few times."

"That's all?"

"For Pete's sake, the theater, a movie now and then. What difference does it make?"

"It makes a hell of a lot of difference," he said slowly, his eyes narrowed on her face. "No wonder you look so intimate in that photograph. If you're not having an affair with Kowalt, you're well on the way."

"We're friends," she said, her dark eyes beginning to smolder. "He's a sportscaster who's been assigned to cover the Olympic figure-skating team, and I'm one of those team members. We travel the same circuit. Why shouldn't we spend time together?"

"Kowalt is an ex–football player, and what he knows about figure skating could be put in a thimble. If he didn't have Christy Moreno sitting in that box holding his hand and supplying her commentary, he'd make a complete ass of himself."

"He realizes that," she said in defense. "He didn't want the assignment, and he's trying to learn as quickly as he can."

"Well, he can learn from someone else," Anthony said flatly. "Christy Moreno can spend all the time she wants force-feeding him expertise. You're not to see him again."

"I'm not to—" She couldn't believe it. "What earthly right do you think you have dictating my personal life? How would you like me to say, 'You aren't to see Luisa anymore'?" Her eyes were blazing. "It *is* still Luisa, isn't it? Or are you keeping another mistress now? You've had enough women to qualify for a gold in physical endurance over the years."

"Yes, it's still Luisa," he said, his lips tight. "I'm glad you regard my stamina so highly, but I assure you there's no strain, only pleasure, in that particular sport."

"I wouldn't know," she said through clenched teeth. She stood up and leaned forward, her hands resting lightly on the mahogany desk. "But if I decide to broaden my base of experience in that area, you can be sure I'll do it. I'll accept your orders in my professional life, but I'll be damned if I'll let you tell me who to see and not to see."

"Or who to go to bed with?" he asked silkily.

"Exactly. It's none of your concern."

"It's very much my concern," he said with soft menace. "Your ex-quarterback will find that out if he tries to call any plays that I regard as foul." His silver-green eyes weren't cold but hot now, Dany noticed. "I'm trying to hold on to my patience until after Calgary, Dany, but I'd advise you not to push me. Don't see him again."

"I don't know what you're talking about," she said angrily. "I haven't understood half the allusions you've made today. You're not acting like yourself at all."

"Aren't I?" He smiled, a slash of brilliance that didn't quite reach his eyes. "But how would you know, Dany? You've never known me. Not really."

She knew that, and it was an aching emptiness inside her. "You haven't let me." Her voice was shaking with confusion and anger. "You've never let anyone close enough for that."

He became still. "I know," he said quietly. "And it's time for a change. I plan to let you come as close to me as you want to from now on. But I've waited so long, it's made me a little savage. We only have a little further to go. Please don't stretch my patience to the breaking point." He paused. "Cross Jack Kowalt off your list."

"Just like that?" She snapped her fingers. "Why should I?" She could feel her throat tighten with tears. "He gives me warmth and friendship and makes me feel I'm something special. Not only as a skater, but as a woman." She drew a deep, quivering breath. "Why should I give that up because you've suddenly decided you're generously going to allow me to be your friend? You might change your mind tomorrow and decide I'm not worthy of you. I don't think you'd make a very reliable friend, Anthony."

There was a flicker in his eyes that in another man might have been interpreted as pain. "We'll have to see, won't we? I don't think I've been a bad friend to you for the past fourteen years."

"You've given me everything," she said huskily. "Almost everything." She turned and walked toward the door. She faced him again and her eyes were suspiciously bright. "Where were you yesterday? I *needed* you."

He shook his head. "No, you didn't. You don't need anyone. Remember that."

He was wrong. She'd needed him and he hadn't been there. "We're not all as strong as you are, Anthony," she said, lifting her chin proudly. "And we're not all made out of ice."

"You're stronger than you think. Someday you'll find that out." His lips tightened. "And if it makes you feel any happier, at the moment I don't feel anything close to being a man made of ice."

"Where were you?" she persisted.

He parted his lips to speak but restrained his words. Then, his face impassive, he said, "As you told the commentator, I'm a busy man."

The pain was swift and piercing. "You see? You wouldn't make a very good friend," she said shakily. "Friends understand you and are there when you need them, Anthony." She turned, her hand on the doorknob.

"Dany."

She paused, waiting.

"I understand you better than anyone in this whole damn world." His words vibrated with force. "And I never said I wanted to be your friend."

Chapter 2

Dany closed the door behind her and leaned back against it for a long moment. Her heart was beating wildly, and fear, bewilderment, and an odd excitement were racing through her veins. That last, enigmatic statement couldn't have meant what it sounded like. Anthony had never exhibited the slightest interest in her as anything but a protégée, a Galatea for his Pygmalion. No, it couldn't be a sexual attraction that had made him behave so strangely tonight.

But if it had been? The excitement and panic increased by giant proportions. She wouldn't know how to cope with the type of sexual chemistry

Anthony generated so effortlessly. Her feelings for him were so intense and confused, she couldn't possibly sort them out. Admiration, hero worship, resentment, dependence. Love? Yes, that was there too. She'd loved Anthony all her life, and it had been a love that only fed the resentment. There couldn't be any more hurtful or frustrating emotion on the face of the earth than loving Anthony Malik, with his leashed stillness and the veil of ice crystals he kept firmly between himself and the world.

A sexual relationship with Anthony, Dany mused. Oh, Lord, it would destroy her. Ice could burn, and Anthony had the reputation for keeping his ladies very contented—for as long as he kept them. However, his passion for them always cooled.

She wouldn't be able to stand it if, with time, he grew bored and decided she wasn't what he wanted after all. He might even decide to shut her out of his life entirely! She felt the panic rise up within her. She couldn't imagine an existence without Anthony hovering in the background like a dark, enigmatic shadow. Strong, incisive, always in control. What would he be like if he lost that control? She felt her breasts tauten beneath her sweater and a strange ache begin between her thighs. Desire.

No! Her relationship with Anthony was too complicated already. She hurried down the hall, her face flushed as if she had a fever. She'd felt that aching melting once before. Six years before, and it had gotten her thrown out of Eden. Anthony had seen it and had rejected her with his usual implacable decisiveness. She wouldn't risk a second rejection.

Pete Drissell was coming down the curving staircase as she snatched up her beige polo coat from the bench where she'd left it. "I've just taken your bags up to your room, Miss Alexander."

"Good," she said absently as she shrugged into her coat. "I'm sorry to inconvenience you again, Pete, but I wonder if you'd drive me back to New York? I know it's a long trip, but I'd really appreciate it. Something's come up that I need to take care of." It wasn't a total falsehood; she had to banish this panic and emotional turmoil before she saw Anthony again. Her nerves were screaming with tension, and she knew she wouldn't be able to sit across from him at the dinner table in a few hours without falling apart. She needed breathing space.

There was surprise on the chauffeur's face but his reply was impeccably courteous. "Certainly. No trouble at all. Shall I get one of your suitcases from your room?"

She shook her head. "I'll probably only be gone overnight. I'll pick up something in New York if I need it." She didn't want to wait for anything. She just wanted to get away before she saw Anthony again, before she had to face something she wasn't sure she'd ever be able to handle. She had to regain a portion of that serene poise Anthony had shattered and soothe the raw nerve endings that her own emotional upheaval had brought to the surface. She tied the belt of her polo coat, picked up her shoulder bag, and hurried out the front door, a puzzled Pete Drissell following close behind.

* * *

"Are you going to talk about it?" Jack Kowalt asked quietly as he filled her coffee cup from the carafe the waitress had just set on the red-checked tablecloth. His warm brown eyes were narrowed on her face. "Or am I going to be the polite dinner companion and ignore the fact that you're upset as hell about something?"

"You're supposed to ignore it," Dany said, forcing a smile. "After all, why spoil your record? You didn't even bat an eyelash when I showed up on your doorstep and whisked you off to dinner."

"I was afraid you'd change your mind." In the rawboned toughness of his face his crooked grin was boyishly appealing. "It's not often that I see you display any signs of aggressiveness in our relationship. It's very restful just to sit back and let a liberated woman make the moves."

"Is it?" She wrinkled her nose at him. "You may have to coach me a little in the role. I don't know much about the liberation movement. I'm afraid I've always been too busy to pay much attention to it."

"So I understand." He looked down at his coffee thoughtfully. "Before I got this assignment, I never realized how much dedication and work you skaters had to put into the sport. It boggles the mind. How long have you been at it?"

"In competition since I was ten, but I started skating when I was four." She added cream to her coffee and stirred it slowly, her dark eyes pensive. "There's a large pond on the grounds at Briarcliff, and my parents used to invite their friends to skating parties in the winter. I used to sneak out of my room at night and watch them sometimes. I'd hide in the trees and sit for hours watching the tall, handsome men and pretty, graceful girls gliding around the pond as if they had wings." She smiled, her face soft with memories. "It was all touched with magic. The moonlight turned the ice to glittering silver. There were tall wrought-iron torches on the banks, and they were mirrored on the surface, as if the flames were captured beneath the ice. The first time I saw Anthony, he reminded me of one of those torches. He was wearing a black sweater and jeans and he moved over the pond like a dark flame, spinning, attacking the ice." She glanced up at him. "Have you ever seen Anthony skate?"

"Once. When he won the gold at the Olympics. He's very good."

"He's more than that. He's the most incredibly graceful skater I've ever watched. And the power and passion he brings to it are unbelievable. He's absolutely superb, both technically and artistically." She shook her head. "Of course, I didn't realize that at the time. All I remember is wondering rather whimsically why he didn't burn those other skaters as he brushed past them. He wasn't like the rest of them at all. Everyone else was so happy. There was so much laughter. At other parties I'd seen, no one *touched* anyone else. Even when they were dancing they were alone somehow. But not when they were skating." She shrugged helplessly. "It's hard to explain."

"You've done very well," he said gently. "So you learned to skate so you'd be able to join those parties?"

She shook her head. "I knew they'd never let me do that." Her lips twisted. "My parents believed children should be relegated to the nursery until they reached a civilized age. No, I only wanted to snatch a bit of that magic for myself. I nagged my nanny unmercifully until she saw that I was supplied with skates and lessons. She wasn't any too pleased with the results, as I remember. She hated sitting on the bank in the freezing cold while I practiced. She couldn't get me away from the ice once I'd started. It became an obsession with me." She glanced up to meet his sympathetic eyes and gave her head a little shake as if to clear it. "It still is."

"You practice six or seven hours a day on the ice and then have two hours of ballet when you've finished that," he said slowly. "I've seen you so tired, you could scarcely put one foot in front of the other, and yet you still kept on working. Is it worth it, Dany?"

"Yes, it's worth it," she said, her tone very steady. "I've always known that. Why do you think I do it?"

"I've sometimes wondered." He took a sip of his coffee. "I thought perhaps it might be Malik."

She tensed. "You sound like those idiotic newspaper stories they've been writing about me for the past two years. Ever since I won the World Championship, the columnists have been trying to read something diabolically Machiavellian into Anthony's support and help in my career. He's never pushed me into anything. He just very generously gave me the support I needed. If I'm being driven, it's not by him but by my own ambition."

"Okay, okay," he said soothingly, raising his hand. "I wasn't maligning your guardian. I even admire him in a remote sort of way. It's just that I thought he might be giving you a hard time after the competition yesterday."

"He scarcely mentioned it," she said curtly. She didn't want to think of that conversation in the library. She'd come to Jack to take comfort in his warm, easygoing friendliness. She'd thought it might ease the tension that was surging through her, and it had, for a little while. If she didn't think about Anthony, she might be able to push that scene into the background for the rest of the evening. She smiled at Jack with determined cheerfulness. "Now, how about letting me practice my aggressive techniques by asking you to dance on that postage stamp of a floor?"

It was almost midnight when they left the basement bistro. The winter wind was sharp and clean against her warm cheeks and a light snow was falling.

Jack drew the collar of his suede jacket up around his throat and took her hand. "This snow wasn't supposed to start until morning. It's going to be hell getting a taxi. They always disappear into the great beyond at the first sign of bad weather."

"Your apartment building isn't all that far. Why don't we walk? I could use some fresh air."

"My apartment?" Jack's brows lifted inquiringly. "Now that's *my* kind of aggressiveness. You're doing better all the time, Dany. You're staying the night?"

"No, I'm going to let you give me a cup of hot chocolate after our walk." She tucked her arm through his and started off briskly. "Then I'm going to use your telephone to call around to find a hotel room and wait in comfort until a taxi appears from the great beyond to take me to said hotel."

"If you're going to wait for that, you may stay the night after all." He grinned down at her. "My bed is yours." He winked. "Also my magnificent body, which sold for two million dollars when I turned pro. How can you turn down an offer like that? It's just not good business sense."

"I was always lousy at business affairs. I leave that to the experts like Anthony."

The snow falling on his sandy hair blended into it and became invisible. Anthony's hair was so sable-dark, snowflakes always appeared starlike in contrast, Dany thought. She bit her lip and deliberately forced the image out of her mind. She'd almost forgotten Anthony in the last few hours, and it was going to stay that way.

As it turned out, it stayed that way only until they were half a block from Jack's apartment building. The lights of a gray Mercedes parked across the street flicked on and the car made a screeching U-turn that was met by a riotous burst of honking from the other cars on the street. It glided to a smooth stop beside Dany, and the driver leaned over to fling open the passenger door.

"Get in, Dany." Anthony's face was pale and taut under the Mercedes' dome light, his eyes hard silver with anger. "As you can see, I'm holding up traffic. I've already gotten one ticket this evening waiting for you to show up. I don't want another one." His gaze moved to Jack with a glittering ferocity that caused the sportscaster's face to cloud with bewilderment. "I'm sure you'll understand why Dany has to cut the evening short, Kowalt. She's under a strict training regimen and needs all the rest she can get." His tone became silky. "You're an ex-athlete yourself, so you know how the kind of activity you have in mind can sap the strength."

"Anthony!" Dany's voice was indignant. "You have no right to say—"

There was a loud honking from the van in back of the Mercedes and Anthony's voice took on a steel-sharp edge. "Get in, Dany. *Now.*"

She'd obviously have to if she didn't want Anthony to cause a major traffic jam, she thought crossly. She squeezed Jack's arm with swift affection before releasing it. "I'd better go," she said. "I'll give you a call tomorrow." She slipped into the passenger seat of the Mercedes and slammed the door shut. "Let's go. You're going to have that van ramming you in a minute."

"It wouldn't surprise me," Anthony said as he coolly pulled away from the curb into the stream of traffic. "Anyone would have to be crazy to drive in New York in a snowstorm."

"Then why are you doing it?" she asked tightly. "Why are you here at all? I wasn't running away from home like an irresponsible child. I would have been back at Briarcliff tomorrow."

"I wasn't concerned about tomorrow." He darted her a glance that was colder than the snow blowing against the windshield. "I didn't want you spending the night in Kowalt's bed."

"I'll spend my nights anywhere I please," she said crisply. "I won't account to you for anything but my professional life, Anthony. I thought I'd made that clear."

"Evidently I didn't make myself equally clear," he said. "But I intend to. Before this night's through, you're going to understand our entire situation a hell of a lot better."

"Are we going back to Briarcliff?"

"Not in this weather. I'm no masochist, though I've been acting like one for some time. We'll stay at my apartment in town."

"I'd rather go to a hotel," Dany said, her eyes fixed stubbornly on the windshield wipers. "If you'll drop me off, I'll see you back at Briarcliff tomorrow afternoon."

"Be quiet, Dany," Anthony said with barely controlled anger. "I've had a bitch of a day since Pete got back to Briarcliff after dropping you off on Kowalt's doorstep like a too-eager call girl. I don't want you to goad me into losing my temper. Not tonight."

"You're being your usual autocratic self, Anthony. Didn't it occur to you that's why I decided to get away from you for a while?"

"It occurred to me," he said grimly. "It also occurred to me that I'd probably scared you right into Kowalt's bed." He flipped on his turn signal and drove into the underground parking lot beneath a towering modern structure that appeared to be composed principally of shimmering smoked glass. "I was a little uptight or I'd never have made that mistake." He pulled into a parking space and shut off the ignition before turning to her with a mirthless smile. "You can be sure it's not one I'll make again after the hell I've been through tonight. So forget about getting away from me. I'm not about to let you do it again. Not for an hour, much less a night." She parted her lips to speak, her dark eyes smoldering, but he was opening the door and stepping out of the car. "Come on, you can let all that indignation loose on me when we get up to the apartment."

She'd do just that, she decided, as she watched him turn his key in the electric lock of the elevator and press the floor button. She had been frightened and unsure before, just as he'd guessed, but that was subdued now by anger.

Anthony's apartment was so completely different from Briarcliff that she stopped in surprise just inside the door. It was all sleek, modern lines and boldly masculine decor. Blue-gray walls and matching carpet contrasted with the midnight-blue velvet couch and chairs. Even the chrome-tiled fireplace in the sunken living room was stark and modern. The logs lit with a touch of Anthony's finger on the gas starter as he knelt before it.

"It's so different," she said as she took off her coat and dropped it on an easy chair. "It's not like Briarcliff at all."

He stood up and shrugged out of his jacket. "Why should it be? Briarcliff is your home, not mine. Old money, antiques, cozy warmth. None of those are me."

He was right; there was nothing cozy about Anthony. "No money, old or otherwise," she said tersely. "I've had the fact of your subsidizing me rubbed in often enough by the media."

"There was plenty of money before your parents decided that palatial yachts and parties at twenty thousand a clip were de rigueur for their pleasure." He picked up her coat and moved across the foyer to hang it up neatly along with his in the hall closet. "They should have set up a trust fund to protect you in case something happened to them."

"We don't all plan and plot our lives to the last detail," she said defiantly. "They were happy. And, if I recall, you attended a good many of those parties. I remember seeing you any number of times."

"Yes, you would." There was a curiously tender curve to his lips. "From behind the potted plants at the head of the stairs or peeping out around that white birch tree by the pond. I used to worry

49

about you getting too cold, but you seemed to be bundled up warmly."

"Yes, I was always warm enough," she said absently. "You knew I was there watching? I didn't think anyone noticed."

"Perhaps I wouldn't have if I hadn't been so god-awful bored and looking for a distraction." He took her arm and propelled her down the three steps into the sunken living room and over to the couch before the fireplace. "I'd just won the Olympic gold and was the star of an ice show. I suppose I was curious to taste all the delights of fame and adulation." He dropped down on the couch. "It got old very fast. I wasn't used to people making pleasure their prime motivation for existence. I got so I looked forward to seeing your fiery red hair and grave dark eyes behind that potted palm. Once you weren't there, and it bothered me all evening. I couldn't ask Nan or Jeffrey because obviously they didn't realize you were spying on them. I finally cross-examined one of the servants and found you were sick with a virulent case of the flu." His lips tightened. "Not that it changed any of your parents' social plans. They didn't even try to keep the noise down at the party."

Dany sank down into the deep armchair across from the couch. "You sound like you didn't even like them," she whispered, her eyes enormous in her thin face.

"I didn't," he said bluntly, leaning back against the midnight-blue velvet cushions. "They were selfish, egotistical, lazy, and even a little stupid. I disliked them as much as the crowd they surrounded themselves with."

"Of which you were part," she said tartly. "You didn't have to go to their parties if you didn't like them."

"I was a little lost." His silver-green eyes were thoughtful as they stared into the fire. "I was only twenty years old, and after working and struggling all my life, I suddenly had it all. Money, fame, women—everything I wanted was laid at my feet." His lips twisted bitterly. "And I discovered that I didn't really want any of it. It wasn't enough."

Her troubled eyes widened. "Is that how it's going to be for me?" she asked, biting her lip.

"After all the work and worry, is it all going to be empty?"

"No." His answer was reassuringly swift. "We're as different as night and day. Darkness and sunlight. You love skating. It's part of you and always will be. It enhances and completes you." He met her eyes steadily. "It was never that to me. I used it to escape from poverty and from being a victim. It was the only emotional outlet I allowed myself when I was growing up. I knew that emotion must exist or the skating had no depth or color." He shrugged. "Then, after I'd gained all the rewards I'd worked for, I found I didn't like the idea of displaying my emotions for the audience's delectation." He paused. "I'm not a very generous man, Dany. I'm much more likely to take than give."

"Why are you telling me all of this?" His expression was set and tense, almost pained, and she knew he wouldn't ordinarily reveal anything like this about himself.

"Because it's necessary," he said gratingly. "Do you think I'm enjoying this? I don't know how to open up and let anyone get close to me. But I have to let you in, dammit."

"Why?"

"Because if I don't, you're going to fall into Kowalt's bed." He paused. "And then I'll probably kill him."

The words were said with deadly impassivity that was more frightening than anger. She shivered. "You can't mean that."

"I mean it," he said. "When did I ever say anything to you I didn't mean? That's why I brought you here. I have to make sure you understand what you're dealing with." He closed his eyes, and for a moment there was a look of unutterable weariness on his face. "I don't want to hurt you, Dany. That's the last thing I want. But it's been so damn *long*." His eyes opened, and there was a glimmer of pain in their depths. "Too long. I can't wait anymore."

"Wait for what?" Her throat was so tense, she could scarcely get out the words.

"You," he said simply. "It's always been you."

She shook her head in instinctive rejection.

"No." She wrapped her arms about herself to still her trembling. "It's not possible, you never said—"

"I told you it wasn't easy for me to show my feelings," he said harshly. "That doesn't mean I don't have them. I've known ever since you were a little girl that you were going to be mine someday. Mine in all the ways there are. Since the night I first spoke to you. Do you remember that evening, Dany?" He shook his head impatiently. "How could you? You were only six years old." He gazed unseeingly into the flames. "It was snowing that day too. There was a cocktail party going on inside, and I was feeling practically claustrophobic, so I got my jacket and decided to walk down to the pond to get some air. You were dressed in jeans and a white wool sweater, and your ponytail was like a flame as you practiced your spins on the ice. You looked so grave and intent, yet there was more warmth and vitality in you than I'd ever seen in a human being before. Snowflakes were falling all about you. It was almost twilight and you shone like a bright beacon. I stood on the bank just watching you, and then you saw me and came skating over."

Anthony's lips curved in reminiscence. "You smiled at me and said, 'I know who you are. You're Anthony Malik and you won a gold medal. I'm Dany Alexander and one day I'm going to win one too. And then everyone will love me.'" He looked up from the flames to meet her eyes. "I knew then that one person already . . . cared for you and was going to for the rest of his life." His hands clenched involuntarily. "And I knew that it was going to be hell on earth waiting for you to get through all the years that kept us apart. I've never been a patient man, Dany."

"That's crazy." She shook her head in bewilderment. "Things don't happen like that."

"I didn't think so either." His lips twisted in a sardonic smile. "You couldn't ask for a more cynical or pragmatic man than I was at that time. I believed I could fashion the world and everything in it to suit myself. Needless to say, it came as something of a shock to run across fate in the form of a six-year-old imp who thought of me as just another grown-up."

"It doesn't make any sense," she repeated dazedly. "Why me?"

He shrugged. "I just knew you were the only one who could complete me," he said haltingly, as if the words were difficult to get out. "I told you I couldn't release emotion like other people. I've never been able to care for anyone. You weren't far wrong when you accused me of being an iceman. You were everything that I wasn't: warm, open, giving." He paused. "Loving. I wanted that warmth, that love. I knew it then and I know it now."

"I can't—"

"I'm not asking you to love me," he said gravely. "I realize I'm not an easy person to love. You may even find it impossible. I'm just telling you I want it. There are other things that we can give each other. I'm not trying to wring any commitments from you. I just want you to know that you're going to belong to me and that you're going to *want* to belong to me."

"You can't force emotions like that," she said huskily. Her chest was tight, and it was painful even to breathe.

"I don't intend forcing anything," he said with composure. "You're going to come to me of your own free will. You're going to want to be in my arms as much as I want you there. Did you think I'd want anything else?" He shook his head, a slight smile curving his lips. "No gratitude, no obligation, no fear." His intent glance caught her slight stiffening at the last word, and his voice deepened to gentleness. "Yes, I've always known you were a little afraid of me. I suppose it was instinctive. You could sense the intensity of what I was feeling even if you couldn't understand it. There was so much warmth in you that perhaps you were even afraid if you came too near, I'd extinguish that flame." There was a fitful spark in his eyes. "I won't do it, you know. If anything, I'm liable to burn you up." He stretched out his hand. "Come here and see."

His eyes were glowing softly, not glittering as they usually were, and they held her own with mesmerizing force. His expression was gentle and more vulnerable than she'd ever seen it. She stood up and moved with a dreamlike lethargy to stand before him. Still holding her gaze, he turned his palm upward. "Come," he coaxed, and hesitantly she put her hand in his.

She almost jerked it back as she felt the warm, throbbing electricity that seemed to leap between them, but his hand had closed securely around her own. "See, nothing to be afraid of. What you feel is only what's always going to happen between us from now on. It's kind of a melting, one into the other."

"You're speaking to me as if I were a little girl," she said. The firelight was playing across the boldness of his high cheekbones, and she could see it mirrored in his eyes. She had a fleeting memory of a torch's flame captured within moonlit ice, and she felt suddenly breathless.

He parted his legs and with a gentle tug pulled her to the floor so that she was kneeling between them. "I know you're not a little girl." He leaned forward, and she could see the sudden cadence of his heartbeat in the hollow of his throat. "Sometimes when you're frightened or disturbed about something, you lift your chin so proudly that your throat arches like that of a startled gazelle." His thumb rested lightly on that pulse point, feeling the erratic fluttering. "Lovely."

"I don't know why I'm letting you do this." She

moistened her lips nervously. "I think I must be crazy too. I was so angry at you only a little while ago."

"You're letting me do it because you want it." He tilted her head, cradling her cheeks in his hands to gaze down into her eyes. "You may have managed to smother it beneath a landslide of other emotions, but you want me too, Dany." His fingertips were brushing lazily over her cheekbones. "Sometimes I believe I'm so sensitive to what you're thinking and feeling that it's as if I'm inside of you looking out." His thumbs moved down to part her lips, rubbing against the warm moisture of her tongue. "I could tell the very minute you began to want me. You were confused and scared, but the wanting was there." He drew a deep, shuddering breath. "I was teaching you pair skating and we were working on that overhead split. My hands were on your inner thigh, supporting you. I'd held you like that a thousand times but suddenly something changed. You tensed beneath my hand, and I glanced up and you were looking down at me, and it was all there in your face." His thumb moved lazily over the edge of her teeth. "I felt as if someone had punched me in the stomach. I'd been still thinking of you as a child, and there you were with that look in your eyes that meant I could have you, that I could teach you to belong to me as a woman."

"You sent me away from Briarcliff," she said haltingly. "I could see by your expression I'd given myself away. I thought I had made a complete fool of myself."

He shook his head. "It was either send you away or ruin everything I'd waited for." His voice was harsh with frustration. "You were only fourteen, for heaven's sake! If I'd kept you with me, you'd have been my mistress by the time you were sixteen. I wouldn't have been able to help myself."

No, Dany thought, and she wouldn't have been able to help herself either. She'd been trying to blot out that painful memory from her consciousness for the last six years, yet he had only to touch her as he was doing now and she remembered the deep throbbing ache for completion she'd known that afternoon when she'd crossed the boundary from childhood to womanhood. "It won't work, you know," she said, closing her eyes as she felt the waves of heat wash over her. "We can't found a relationship on something as insubstantial as desire. As you said, we're complete opposites."

"We can start there." His thumb was beneath her tongue, urging it to venture from her lips. "I feel a hell of a lot more than desire, but I can accept that from you and build on it." He slowly lowered his head, his warm lips rubbing sensuously against her tongue. "I'll try to make it so good for you, it won't matter to you if you can't feel anything deeper for me." He inhaled deeply. "Now, hush. I want to kiss you, taste you."

His lips closed slowly, carefully on hers, fitting and blending with a gentleness that was all the more moving for the leashed savagery she could sense beneath it. His breath was warm and minty. His tongue, as it licked teasingly at the corner of her mouth and then traced the fullness of her lower lip, was exquisitely arousing. He raised his head and drew a deep, shaky breath. "Do you know how often I've wanted to do that? How I've lain awake and wondered how you'd taste? How you'd feel? I've known your body so well over the years. I've handled you, held you in my arms, even made a parody of love to you on ice, but I've never felt you respond to me as a woman. *Respond,* Dany. Lord, I need that." She could feel his heart thundering under the rough wool of his sweater as he drew her head to rest against it. "I want my hands on you," he whispered into her hair. "Will you let me touch and learn you?"

Her heart jerked. "I don't know." It was all happening too swiftly. She felt as if she were drifting through a sensual dream. The warmth of the fire, the roughness of his sweater against her cheek, the scent of clean soap, the *feel* of him. How long had she wanted him to hold her like this and suppressed it into oblivion? It seemed as if it must have been a lifetime. Now he was here, not remote, not cold, wanting her. It was too much. "I think you're right. I think I *am* afraid of you."

"That's why you should let me love you." His hand was moving deftly in her hair, removing the pins that held her bun in place. "Then you'll know there's nothing to be afraid of. The last thing I want to do is hurt you." Her auburn hair tumbled down her back in a shimmering cloud, and he threaded his hands through it with lazy sensuality. "I'm not going to rush you. I know what pressures you're going to be under for the next month, and there's no way I'm going to ask you for a final commitment until you're clear of that." One hand was beneath her hair, massaging the coiled tension at her nape. "We're just going to learn each other's bodies." His lips touched her temple. "You're going to find out how much I want you and you're going to want me too." His teeth nibbled at her ear. "You're going to sleep naked in my arms so that you'll know you belong to me as I belong to you. And that there's no possibility of either one of us belonging to anyone else from now on."

His teeth moved down to pull gently at her lower lip. "I wanted to wait but I couldn't have you turning to Kowalt because I hadn't shown you how sweet it's always going to be between us." His lips fastened hungrily on hers and he gave a groan deep in his throat as he kissed her with almost frantic urgency. His hands were suddenly on her hips, moving the thigh-length sweater up her body. He dragged his mouth from hers and pushed her body a little away, and then the sweater was over her head and tossed carelessly aside. He held her startled gaze with his own as his hands moved to the front clasp of her bra.

In the beige lace bra Dany was all soft gold and shimmering ruby in the firelight, her eyes dark with bewilderment and desire. Anthony's hands were shaking slightly as he undid the clasp, and he drew a long, shuddering breath. Careful, he told himself. He had to be careful not to show her the need that was tearing him apart. He could feel himself harden and the muscles of his stomach clench painfully. He wanted to tear off her clothes, throw her on the floor, and bury himself in her. Damn, he wanted that. The thought of her legs curving around him, her body arching to him, her dark eyes staring up at him clouded with desire, was driving him berserk.

He'd been so sure he could keep control of the situation. His lips curved in a mirthless smile as he remembered how he'd assured her he wouldn't ask for a final physical commitment. He knew she wasn't ready for that yet. This was all too new and bewildering for her. He'd happily mutilate Kowalt for precipitating his plans. He'd wanted to wait. No, he'd felt it would be fairer to Dany to wait—wanting had nothing to do with it. He'd been in a blaze of heated need for Dany since that afternoon six years ago. Fourteen years old. Lord, he'd felt as shocked and disgusted with himself as if he'd actually taken her instead of sending her away. He'd tried to smother it beneath the tenderness and love he'd felt for her since the first moment he'd seen her, but every so often he'd feel a stab of desire so intense, it had been actual pain. He'd constantly reinforced his vigilance but he'd known it was there, just waiting to burst free. And was he supposed to keep that passion under control while he teased them both into a frenzy? He would have to if he hoped to block Kowalt from her mind and still leave her free. Hell, Anthony told himself, what was a little more torture after what he'd gone through for the past six years?

He parted the bra and slipped the straps slowly over her shoulders. Lord, she was beautiful. Small, but perfectly formed, her breasts tilting up perkily with the deep pink rosettes hardening even as he looked at her. Hardening for him. He could feel the swelling in his loins reach painful proportions as he watched her body flush and tauten, readying itself for his touch, his possession.

"Come to me," he said thickly. "Please, Dany. I want to kiss them, love them." He was drawing her from her knees onto his lap and he could see her eyes widen as she felt the evidence of his bold arousal against her. It didn't frighten her though, thank heaven. It only caused her eyes to darken to midnight softness and her pulse to accelerate in the hollow of her throat. She was so responsive, Anthony thought. His eyes narrowed as he arched her up to rub those beautiful, sensitive breasts against the rough wool of his sweater. She gave a little gasp, and he could feel her tense.

"No, don't. It hurts."

He froze, his gaze flying down to meet her eyes in surprise. He'd purposely kept the caress feather-light. "Hurts?"

"No." She shook her head in confusion. "Not hurts. Burns. I don't know. I can't *stand* it." She felt as if her heart were going to burst through her chest. How could she explain the wild, heated sensation that had flamed through her, sending out signals to every part of her body? Signals she didn't understand. But Anthony understood. She could tell by the way his lips were curving tenderly as he looked down at her.

"Too rough?" he asked. "Let's see if we can find them something softer to nestle against." He pushed her away a little and swiftly pulled off his sweater and tossed it aside. He rapidly unbuttoned the black shirt beneath it. When it was completely unfastened, he paused. His eyes were glowing silver in the firelight as he urged her quietly, "Take it off me, Dany. *Take* what you want."

Take what you want. The philosophy was easy for Anthony to expound. He'd always taken what he wanted from life with a bold incisiveness. But he wasn't taking now; he was giving.

Her hands came hesitantly up to his shoulders and closed on the dark cotton of his shirt. She gave a shuddering sigh and her eyes closed as she slowly slid the shirt from his shoulders and down his arms. The hard tips of her breasts swung gently against his hair-roughened chest with the movement, and she heard Anthony's harsh inhalation as her head sank to rest against him. His heart was thundering explosively against her ear, and she rubbed her cheek back and forth with the sensuousness of a cat. He smelled so good. Slightly spicy with a musk base that was all clean, virile male. She wanted to stay here forever just breathing in the fresh vitality of him. She ran her tongue over one hard male nipple. He tasted good too. Slightly salty, yet warm and smooth. Her lips pressed around the hard nub as she sucked gently, feeling a strange primitive enjoyment as the arched tenseness of his muscles increased tenfold.

"I think you'd better stop taking what you want for a bit, sweetheart"—he half-groaned, half-laughed—"or I'm going to be tempted into doing the same." His hand tangled in her hair and he pulled her head back. Her eyes opened with a dreamy languor, and the expression in them made his breath stop. God, how long he'd waited for her to look at him like that. "I think it's time for bed, Dany," he said huskily. "Will you sleep in my arms tonight?"

She nodded slowly, feeling as if the world were narrowing and telescoping to contain only silver-green eyes lit with flames, supple bronze muscles that flexed and moved against her softness with a hunger that was ravishing to the senses. "If you want me to," she whispered.

She'd do anything he wanted her to do. She knew that with a serene certainty now. She was so overflowing with love for him that it filled her with a dreamlike disorientation. Love. She'd been so careful never to think of love in connection with Anthony. It was safe to love Beau and Marta, and she'd given that love freely. It was even easy to give warmth and affection to Jack and the other men who'd faded in and out of her life. With Anthony it was different. She'd never known what he was feeling behind that wall of reserve. But she'd wanted to know. Oh, Lord, how she'd wanted to know! All her life all she'd ever wanted was to look behind that veil into the man that was Anthony Malik. Now, with a suddenness that was incredible, he was lowering the barrier and inviting her in.

"That's not enough," he said quietly. "It's got to be what you want too." His fingers were warm on her naked back, drawing lazy, sensual patterns on its satin softness. "Tell me that you want it, Dany."

His fingers were pulling invisible wires of

sensation that caused a spasmodic clenching between her thighs and a melting hotness in her veins. "I want it," she said huskily in a half gasp. "Oh, yes, I want it, Anthony."

His lips touched hers in a kiss as soft as gossamer wings. "So sweet," he murmured only a breath away. "I suppose I should feel like a bastard taking advantage of an innocent like you, but I don't. You were meant to be mine. You'll know that soon, even if you don't know it now."

Then he was rising, scooping her up in his arms, carrying her up the three steps that led from the sunken living room and across the corridor. He didn't bother to shut the door as he entered the bedroom, and the flickering firelight revealed a room furnished in silver-gray and wine. The deep-piled wine carpet contrasted with the silver-gray of the bedspread on the king-size bed. Then she was being lowered onto that bed's cushioned softness, and the only thing she was conscious of was Anthony standing before her, a slim powerful shadow in the dim room. His hands were rapidly unfastening his belt and his voice was as velvet-soft as the coverlet caressing her naked back. "I've lain on that bed so many nights thinking of how it would be when you were lying there with me." He was stripping with lithe swiftness. Every move was imbued with an inherent economy and grace. She loved to watch him move—on the ice or sprawled in a chair or walking across a room. He was finished now, and his nude body had a gleaming bronze patina that glowed flamelike in the dimness. He sat down beside her and began pulling off her soft suede boots.

"Sometimes I could almost see you with your red hair tumbling over the pillow and your dark eyes looking up at me, pleading for me to love you." He moved up a little on the bed and skillfully slid down the camel slacks and tiny bikini panties beneath them over her hips in one smooth movement. "I'd visualize you opening your thighs, arching up to me and inviting me to—"

"Anthony, it may be dark in here, but I assure you my cheeks are bright scarlet," Dany interrupted shakily. "I'm not accustomed to pillow talk, dammit."

His hand reached out to the crimson-shaded lamp on the bedside table, and they were suddenly in an intimate pool of light that came as a breath-less little shock. He was so beautiful, she thought dreamily, so slender, yet with that gleaming ripple of muscle that invited her touch. And his eyes . . . torches flaming beneath the ice. Those torches were burning her with a hunger that caused the muscles in her stomach to knot as they ran over her with lingering deliberation.

"I've seen you almost naked any number of times," he said thickly. "But not like this. I remember last year in Chicago after that benefit exhibition I came into your dressing room while Marta was giving you a massage with just a scrap of a sheet over you. I sat there across the room talking with Beau, but I couldn't keep my eyes off Marta's hands moving over you with such clinical detachment." He drew a deep, shaky breath. "It drove me crazy. I wanted it to be me touching you, causing that expression of sensual contentment on your face. I had to get the hell out of there or I'd have told them to leave and taken you right there on that table." His eyes lifted from his intimate appraisal of her body to meet her eyes fiercely. "And it wouldn't have been rape, Dany. I'd have given you so much pleasure, you would have been begging for it. I'd never have taken without giving. Not with you. It wouldn't have been possible. Do you understand that?"

She understood that she was melting and dissolving beneath those molten eyes and that the ache between her thighs was close to pain. Every breath she drew was being forced from lungs constricted with a mounting tension that was almost unbearable. "Yes, I can understand that," she whispered." Please don't talk anymore, Anthony." Her hand moved to caress the sleek coiled muscles of his shoulder. "I need you."

She could feel the muscles suddenly tense beneath her hand and grow rigid, and the expression on his face that had been nakedly vulnerable was now an impassive mask. "No, I told you, you don't need anyone. You're too strong for that kind of dependence." His gaze still holding hers, one strong, sensitive hand reached out to cup her breast in his palm. She could feel her heart leap crazily as the breast swelled to his touch. "You *want* me, just as I want you." His thumb flicked the hard, thrusting nipple, leaving a blazing fire in its wake. "And before long you're going to want me a hell of a lot more. But you don't *need* me. Remember that."

He was wrong, she thought wildly. If this desire was beginning to dominate her every sense, wasn't it stark need? It came so close as to be nearly indistinguishable.

Lord, he marveled, she was beautiful lying there with her eyes cloudy and languid, and her lips parted and inviting. He could feel her ripening under his hand, and he wanted to close his hand and squeeze gently, making her blossom even more. He wanted to run his hand over her body, discovering all the softness and textures of her. Her thighs were so damn soft and welcoming. All he had to do was to part those thighs and move between them. She was ready for him. She wanted him. Why the devil didn't he reach out and take what he'd wanted for so long? It would be sheer, agonizing torture to have her lie all night in his arms and not bury himself in her, not give them the pleasure and relief they both wanted.

He closed his eyes for an instant, shutting out the sight of her. He was rationalizing, and he'd never been one to lie to himself. Dany wanted him because he'd used all his expertise to make sure she did. He could take her now and chance that he could build on that experience, but he knew it was a risk he was reluctant to take. She was confused and uncertain now, and in the clear light of morning that confusion might be transformed into resentment and panic. It was all new to her, and he couldn't expect her emotions to be as clearly focused as his own. No, he could only take so much and no more right now.

Besides, though Anthony couldn't claim many virtues, he'd always prided himself on his fairness. His lips curved with a touch of self-mockery as he wondered just how long that sense of justice would have held up if it hadn't been bolstered by the fear that any irrevocable move on his part might ruin his plans for Dany. Not for any appreciable length of time—if the lightest touch of her hand on his shoulder could make him harden with an urgency he'd known only in the final stages of lovemaking with any other woman.

He opened his eyes, and she was still gazing at him with a glowing languor that made his breath catch in his throat. He quickly reached over and flicked off the light. "Come on, sweetheart, under the covers with you. This is all a little more than I can take at the moment." She obediently moved as his hands and body bade her. He drew back the spread and sheet and covered her carefully before slipping in beside her and taking her in his arms. He could feel himself tremble as she molded herself against him with a responsiveness that caused his heart to leap to his throat. Willing. Great heavens, she was so willing, it was tearing him apart. Her lips brushed against his shoulder and he could smell the light floral perfume she always wore as a strand of her silky hair wafted against his cheek.

He was so still, she could feel the iron rigidity of his muscles as she pressed against him. She'd never known how delicious a hard male body could feel against her own softness. The long muscles of his thighs were lightly furred as they rested between her own smoothness, and just the touch of him generated an excitement of its own. But she wanted more. Why was he so still?

"Anthony." Her lips moved to the hollow of his throat. "Make love to me. I won't say I need you if you don't want me to, but you know damn well I want you so much, I'm going crazy."

"Yes, I know that." She could feel the thunder of his heart. "Do you think I don't feel the same way?" He laughed ruefully. "No, the signs are totally unmistakable in our present situation, aren't they?"

Yes, they were, and she knew a deep sense of satisfaction as she nestled closer. "Well, then?"

He drew a shuddering breath. "I can't," he said hoarsely, his hands splayed across her naked back. He moved them up and down with a compulsive sensuality, loving the feel of her. "I can't, dammit!"

"Can't?" she echoed blankly. She couldn't have understood correctly. He couldn't deny them what they both so obviously wanted.

Strong hands tangled in her hair as he drew her to him with a bone-crushing ferocity. "I told you I wasn't going to ask for any final commitment on your part until after Calgary." He laughed mirthlessly. "Don't you realize that if I took you tonight I'd want to own you totally? I know myself too well. I wouldn't give a damn if I monopolized you to the extent of destroying a dream you've devoted most of your life to. And if I did that, I'd lose you forever. So we wait."

She knew a smoldering anger that was born of frustration. "You could have realized that before," she said tartly. "As usual, you've made all the decisions without consulting me." She was trying to push him away as she spoke. "Well, I think this is one decision that should have been a mutual agreement." She was wriggling determinedly, trying to break his hold. "But perhaps you're right. Maybe this wasn't such a good idea after all."

"Lie still." His voice was raw. "You're driving me out of my mind. I never said it was a good idea, only that it was necessary." With easy strength he turned her so that her back was to him, spoon-fashion. "Intimacy may not be as satisfactory as sex but it's all we've got to build on at the moment." His arms held her immobile with inexorable determination. "Now, relax. You're going to sleep in my arms tonight, and if we both don't go off our rockers from sheer frustration, it may be the first step in bridging that intimacy."

"I want you to let me go," she persisted stubbornly. "You can't always have everything your own way, Anthony."

He almost laughed aloud. He was in actual physical pain, and she was speaking as if his decision were a mere whim. Well, how could he expect her to understand him when he had spent most of his adult life guarding against that very thing? "No, I can't always have everything my own way," he agreed wearily, burying his face in the soft mass of her silky hair. "But tonight it's going to be my way, Dany. Make up your mind to that." *Lord, she feels like flowing satin in my arms,* he thought. "Now go to sleep, sweetheart. That will make it easier for both of us."

Chapter 3

Even before she was totally awake, Dany was conscious of an odd sense of being bereft. Anthony was gone. There were no arms holding her with that possessiveness she'd become so accustomed to in one short night; there would be no dark head on that pillow next to her own. She knew it with a certainty that was verified as soon as she opened her eyes.

She felt a sudden jab of loneliness that sent panic coursing through her. Would it always be like that now, waking without Anthony? He'd wanted to brand her with his seal of possession, and she had an idea he'd done just that.

There was a note propped against the base of the lamp on the bedside table, and she recognized the bold black script even as she slowly sat up and reached for the sheet of paper.

Dany,

I've arranged for Pete Drissell to pick you up at eleven and drive you back to Briarcliff. I'll see you there tomorrow.

Anthony

Not exactly a tender missive, she thought wryly: terse and to the point. Anthony never wasted words. Why was she disappointed that there was no hint of affection? He'd shown her passion, not affection, last night. She wasn't even sure he knew what the emotion was.

She threw aside the covers and got out of bed, tossing the note carelessly on the table. She certainly wouldn't be tucking that into her souvenir box as a loving memento, she thought irritably as she crossed to the bathroom on the far side of the room. Within minutes she was standing beneath the shower, letting the heat and gentle spray soothe the aching tension from her muscles.

It had been a night fraught with desire and the sudden awakening of her own sensuality. Out of that morass of emotions Anthony had woven bonds she might never be able to break. Dany didn't even know if she wanted to break them. Her mind was whirling with such a jumble of thoughts and confusion, it only increased the sensation of panic.

Anthony wanted her, and what Anthony wanted, Anthony took. She'd seen that as an inevitable course of events through all her years with him. But Anthony hadn't taken last night. His restraint had been steel-hard even as she'd felt him tremble with desire against her. And that streak of hardness in him was the element that had frightened her the most. She was defenseless against it because she herself would never be able to be hard with Anthony. She would always melt at the first sign of tenderness from him. He'd spoken words of almost obsessive passion, but did Anthony really know how to love? She couldn't know that because she knew so little of the enigma that was Anthony Malik. It could be very dangerous to release the love she'd stored up for years on the chance he'd respond with equal openness. There was nothing open and free about Anthony, and she might well tear her heart out trying to wrest a response from him that he might never be able to give. No, she must go very slowly and not allow him to arouse her as he'd done last night.

She felt a surge of heat flow through her, and her breasts tautened to sudden ripeness as a memory of last night suddenly came back to her. She'd awakened in the middle of the night to feel Anthony's hands running up and down her body in gentle exploration before cupping her breasts, squeezing with rhythmic force that had caused a burning sensation to tingle between her thighs and made her breath leave her lungs. She could feel his chest move against her back with the force of his labored breathing.

"Anthony?" His name was a mere whisper. She could hardly force a sound past the tightness of her throat.

"Lord, I'm sorry, sweetheart." His voice was low and strained, and she could feel the heat of

him like a burning brand against her skin. "I
didn't mean to wake you. So much for my
strength of will." His lips were buried in her hair.
"You're so soft. I had to have my hands on you."

"It's all right," she said faintly, unconsciously
pressing back against him in an undulating movement. Why was he apologizing? she wondered
dazedly. Didn't he know he was only giving her
what she wanted? What she'd always wanted
from him? "I like it." She'd always found it difficult talking to Anthony, but in this heated darkness it was easy to confess even the most intimate
secrets. "I want you to touch me." Her breath was
coming in little gasps.

"I know you do." There was a touch of grimness in his voice. "And if I weren't such a bastard,
I'd have let you sleep through the night and not
brought you down to share the same hell I'm in."

"Haven't you slept at all?"

His chuckle had a thread of pain in it. "Not
very likely when I'm being burned alive." His
hands closed around her breasts with a sudden
force. "And now you're hurting too. I could feel

the aching in you before you fell asleep. I didn't mean to do that to you. Believe me, Dany."

"I believe you," she said. There was a note of desperate sincerity in his voice that made it impossible to do anything else. "It doesn't matter, just make love to me. That will make everything all right."

"You're wrong. That would screw everything up royally," he said bitterly. "Do you think I wouldn't be inside you right now if I wasn't sure of that?" He exhaled in a sigh that was more of a shudder. "But none of this is your fault. You shouldn't be the one to pay." His fingers were plucking teasingly at her nipples, causing rivers of fire to run to the center of her womanhood. "You *won't* be the one to pay." His cheek pushed aside the weight of her hair, his tongue outlining the curve of her inner ear. "You're so sweet. I love the taste of you." His hands, with a touch as exquisitely sensitive as sunlight on rose petals, moved from her breast to her waist and then slid down over the firmness of her belly to the soft down that guarded her womanhood. "The feel of you. You're going to like this, Dany. Just relax and let me help you." Then his hands were moving deftly between her thighs with an expertise that made her arch back against him as a shaft of electrifying pleasure shot through her.

"Anthony!"

"I said you'd like it." His tongue plunged suddenly deep into her ear and the combination of erotic fingers and warm tongue was like an upsurge of white-hot flame. His voice was a harsh rasp. "Do you know how much it excites me to know I can give you pleasure?"

Then he was touching her in a new and different way with the pad of his thumb, and a low cry broke from her. "Anthony, I can't stand it. It's breaking me apart."

"Shhh, it's all right." His strong teeth were nibbling at the lobe of her ear with a pressure sharp enough to be on the borderline of pain, but it only added to the erotic arousal. "Just let go. I'm right here holding you." His caresses suddenly accelerated with a force and skill that caused a small moan to break from her. "Just let go, love."

The release of tension came with a brilliant burst of sensation that was like nothing she'd ever experienced before. Even when the spasms that rocked her to her foundations subsided, she still found herself shaking and breathless. She drew a deep breath and was startled to hear it turn into a sob. There were tears flowing down her cheeks, and she couldn't seem to stop them.

She heard Anthony's low exclamation, and then he was turning her to face him, her face buried in the rough triangle of hair on his chest. His lips were pressed to the top of her head and he was holding her with a cautious gentleness as if she were infinitely precious. "Don't cry," he said thickly. "Please don't cry. Now I'm the one who's breaking apart. I didn't hurt you, did I? I tried to be careful. I only wanted to help you, love."

"You did," she half-sobbed, half-laughed. "Oh, you did. I don't know why I can't stop the waterworks. It's all so stupid."

"No, it's not." There was a trace of relief in his voice. "It's my fault, I suppose. I've thrown everything at you all at once. You'd have to be some kind of superwoman not to experience a pretty traumatic reaction." He gave her a swift hug. "I'm just grateful I didn't hurt you. Hell, I don't know anything about virgins."

She stiffened as she felt a swift pang. No, he wouldn't be expected to be familiar with the idiotic reactions of the inexperienced, she told herself. His chosen mistresses were always knowledgeable and sophisticated in the extreme. Like Luisa. "No, you didn't hurt me," she said quietly. "You were very gentle."

"I tried to be." His lips brushed her head again. "It wasn't easy when all I wanted to do was to come to you and love you. Can you sleep now?"

"I think so." But he wouldn't be able to rest. She could tell by the tense readiness of his body he still felt the aching frustration from which he'd just relieved her. Oh, Lord, why wouldn't he let her help him? Why wouldn't he take from her? Why did he always have to be so damn strong? She nestled her cheek closer, breathing in the lovely clean smell of him. It wasn't any use fighting him. Anthony always did exactly as he thought best. Perhaps someday she'd be able to convince him the aching incompleteness she felt at his refusal to let her share was even worse than the physical incompleteness she'd known before. "Good night, Anthony."

Dany reached out and turned off the faucets with a decisive motion. All this reminiscing wasn't accomplishing anything. It was only reinforcing the wisdom of going very cautiously where Anthony was concerned. Good heavens, he'd actually had her pleading with him to make love to her last night! Surely that fact alone proved how dangerous a relationship with him would be. He'd dominated her practically all her life, but she wouldn't be able to tolerate that threat to her independence now.

She stepped from the shower stall, plucked a soft terry bath towel from the heated rack, and began to dry herself briskly. No, she'd changed from that hero-worshipping child, and Anthony had to come to terms with it. He had a right to mastermind her career, but her personal life was something else again. How many times over the years had she heard herself described as Galatea to Anthony's Pygmalion and only laughed at the comparison? Now it didn't seem quite so funny when she recalled how pliant she'd been to his every wish since he'd practically kidnapped her from under Jack's very eyes.

Jack. She'd promised to get in touch with him before Anthony had snatched her away so precipitously. Dany wrapped the towel around her and strode with determined swiftness back into the bedroom to attempt to locate the clothing that Anthony had removed so deftly last night.

She'd follow Anthony's orders and return to Briarcliff this afternoon. She had a training regimen to follow, and every minute counted now that Calgary loomed so near. But she'd be damned if she'd be hustled off meekly without giving Jack an explanation for Anthony's rudeness last night. She'd have Pete stop at Jack's apartment before they left the city, and to hell with whether Anthony liked it or not. She wasn't about to let him have his own way about everything. Not any longer.

"You didn't blur that last spin," Beau commented mildly as she skated up to the wrought-iron bench on the bank of the pond where he was lolling with deceptive laziness. "The triple looked good, but as I said . . ."

". . . the spin didn't blur," she finished for him as she sat down beside him. She flinched as the iciness of the bench pierced the thinness of her tights. She shouldn't have worn this short skating skirt when she'd known she'd be outdoors, she thought absently as she bent over to unlace her skates. It was fine when she was skating, but it wasn't the most practical outfit when they had a ten-minute walk back to the house from the pond. "I knew it didn't. That snow last night made the ice rough." She glanced up with a grin. "And that's *not* just an excuse. It really would have had enough speed if the ice had been right."

"I wasn't arguing." Beau picked up her heavy cream-colored wool jacket from the bench and draped it over her shoulders. "I'm just wondering what we're doing out here freezing our butts off and having to put up with poor ice when we could be working in that deluxe indoor rink Anthony had built for you out back of ye old family mansion?" His lips twisted in a grin. "As I recall, it even comes complete with a Zamboni to smooth away that rough ice you've been complaining about."

She avoided those keen hazel eyes as she slipped off her left skate and started unlacing the right. "I felt like working outside today. It was nice having the wind and sun on my face after skating inside for the last few months." She took the other skate off. "Besides, sometimes it's good to have the ice a little rough. It gives you something to fight and overcome."

"And ice is a hell of a lot easier to fight than Anthony, isn't it, Dany?" Beau's voice was as soft as his eyes were sharp. "Did he give you a hard time yesterday? Is that why you ran away?"

"I didn't run away," she denied quickly with a forced laugh. "Despite what you think, I'm not a child who's afraid to face some make-believe bogeyman. I just had an impulse to see the bright lights and yielded to temptation. Don't you ever do that, Beau?"

"Yield to temptation?" He grinned. "All the time, sugar. The devil only has to blow in my ear and I'll follow him anywhere." The smile faded. "That's why I'm a world-class expert on the subject and know when amateurs like you are putting me on. You're too damn self-disciplined to take off like that unless you were pretty upset." He picked up her skates and wiped them carefully with the soft cloth she always carried for that purpose before tucking them in her leather satchel. "And as Anthony disappeared right after you did, I gather he was in pursuit of our Little Nell in high dudgeon." His face was grave. "Throw in the fact that you're as edgy as a cat on a hot tin roof and fighting the ice as if it were your worst enemy, and it adds up to big trouble. I think we'd better talk about it, don't you?"

"No, I don't," she said firmly as she thrust her feet into her short suede boots and stood up. "You're my coach, not my sports psychologist. Anthony didn't think I needed one of those, remember?"

"That's not saying he's right." Beau got up leisurely, taking her elbow in one hand and her satchel in the other as they started off over the hard-packed snow along the winding path. The Tudor house was glowing like an Elizabethan jewel in the fast-falling dusk. "There's something to be said for relieving tension and clearing the way for concentration by using a Freudian father confessor." His eyes were suddenly thoughtful. "I think Anthony would have bought you one of those, too, if he hadn't thought you'd resent that kind of crutch as much as he would. He never could stand the idea of leaning on anyone's strength but his own."

"Why, Beau?" She tried to cover the sudden intensity of her tone with a laugh that was not as light as she would have wished. "Why does he have to be the Rock of Gibraltar and the great god Zeus rolled into one? It'd be a great deal easier for the rest of us poor mortals if occasionally he'd come down from Mount Olympus."

"Did you ever consider it would be a lot more comfortable for him too?" Beau asked quietly. "Perhaps he'd like to come down from the mountain but he doesn't know the path anymore. Mount Olympus must be a hell of a lonely place these days. All the ancient gods and goddesses are gone from the temple."

"That won't wash, Beau," she said. "Nothing

ever stops Anthony from doing something he wants to do."

Beau shrugged. "How do you know that? Anthony's a pretty difficult man to read. I still haven't peeled off more than the top layer, and I've known him since I was a kid of eighteen."

"That long?" Her gaze flew to his face in surprise. "I never realized you'd been friends that long. I know you were in that ice revue together before Anthony took over Dynathe." She calculated swiftly. "That's right, I'd forgotten you'd competed in the Olympics together. You won the bronze that year."

"And Anthony won the gold." He made a face. "Not that anyone expected anything else. He was the undisputed favorite before he even skated out on the ice for the compulsories. Still, it hurt like hell at the time. I had my own dreams of glory." His lips twisted wryly. "I'm probably damn lucky I didn't win the gold. I wasn't the type of man then who could handle the high life with any degree of success. I'd probably have ended up on skid row with a bottle of wood alcohol to keep me warm."

Dany's eyes widened. "I don't understand. Skid row?"

"You didn't notice my passionate attachment for ginger ale?" Beau lifted a mocking brow. "I'm an alcoholic, Dany."

"I didn't know," she murmured, shocked. It seemed impossible that she'd been so self-centered as not to have been aware of such a thing in as close a friend as Beau.

"It's not exactly a weakness you talk about in public," he said. "There are still too many people who don't recognize it as a physical illness." His lips tightened grimly. "I didn't myself until Anthony took me by the scruff of the neck and rubbed my nose in it. Until then I had an image of myself as a decadent southern gentleman with a fatal but romantic flaw. That was much easier to accept for a man of my temperament than being 'sick.' Fortunately Anthony has a way of cutting like a knife through our little self-delusions. Probably because he has none himself."

"Anthony knew you were an alcoholic when he hired you as my coach?"

Beau shook his head. "I was on the wagon by

that time. It's not likely he'd have risked me asso-
ciating so closely with his pride and joy if he
hadn't been sure I would stay that way. He took
me in hand before he left the ice show. He made
me face the problem and put me in a clinic to dry
out. Then he whisked me out of temptation's way
and into the straight and narrow when he decided
to turn over your coaching to someone else."

"He did all that for you?" She shook her head
in dazed disbelief. "You must have been very good
friends."

"As close as Anthony would allow." An ironic
smile tugged at his lips. "I'm sure you're aware
that restriction wouldn't exactly make us bosom
buddies. Actually, after we both signed with the
ice show, we had very little contact. My crowd
was a little too wild for his taste. He preferred
more sophisticated playmates. No one was more
surprised than I that he came galloping to the res-
cue when I was gliding down the path to ruin. The
only reason I can come up with was that I'd been
fairly decent to him when we were both going for
the gold. The other competitors were ready to cut

him to little ribbons—even those on his own team."

"So much for the spirit of the Olympics."

"You couldn't really blame them," Beau said. "They'd worked all their lives for a chance at the big time. The difference between winning the gold and taking the silver is a three-million-dollar-a-year contract versus being just another hundred-and-fifty-thousand-dollar-a-year featured skater with an ice show. Maybe I'd have felt the same if I hadn't always had more money than was good for me anyway. Even so, I was feeling pretty raw myself when he showed up at practice and took over the rink as if he owned it." He shrugged. "Hell, he *did* own it. As soon as I saw him work out, I knew I didn't stand a chance."

"That must have been terribly disappointing for you." Dany's voice was soft with sympathy. "I'm not sure how I'd have reacted under the same circumstances. Anthony had cause to be grateful to you, Beau."

He shook his head. "I just behaved the way any other true southern gentleman would have," he drawled, his eyes more golden then as they twinkled. "We've had practice at being defeated by you arrogant Yankees. Perhaps I didn't want the gold as much as the others did. It wasn't worth trying to psych out another competitor, at least. But of course, it wouldn't have been possible with Anthony. He wasn't about to let anyone close enough to endanger his concentration. But they tried. He was the number-one target."

"Naturally." Her face was troubled as she remembered some of the cattiness and venom she'd had to face herself since she'd reached the top rungs of competition. She'd been protected from a great deal of it by the wall of money and care Anthony had fashioned around her, but it hadn't been enough to filter out all of the jealousy. That went with the territory in any competitive sport. The pressure on Anthony must have been excruciating without anyone to run interference. "He was so terribly alone."

"Not entirely. He had old Samuel Dynathe in his corner, remember." Beau made a face. "I can't say that's the kind of support I would have chosen. A patron like Dynathe only tolerates winners.

The pressure from him must have been even worse than from the other competitors."

"He must have cared something for Anthony," Dany argued. She didn't want to think of Anthony as that vulnerable and alone. Vulnerable? Good heavens, what was she thinking of? Anthony could never be vulnerable. "He left him his entire estate when he died, including the entire Dynathe conglomerate."

"He liked winners," Beau repeated. "I don't think he was a man who cared for anyone in the whole damn world. That company was his blood and guts, and he wanted someone at the helm who'd keep it at the top of the heap. He knew Anthony would do that."

"Yes, there'd be no question that he would assure that," Dany said with a bittersweet smile. "Anthony's definitely a winner. The rest of us are left standing at the post."

"I haven't seen any signs of his trying to smother your initiative," Beau said dryly. "Quite the contrary. And having the Rock of Gibraltar to lean upon can be very comforting on occasion.

You're being pretty rough on him, aren't you, Dany?"

"I have to be." She bit her lip. "I guess it's a defense mechanism. You weren't far off when you said I was afraid of him. I've always felt that if I let down my guard even for a moment, all his determination and forcefulness would just sweep me away . . . that there wouldn't be a particle of my own personality left." Her hand made a little gesture of helplessness and frustration. "Oh, damn, I know that sounds crazy as the devil."

"No, it doesn't." Beau's eyes were fixed thoughtfully on her face. "I can see how being Anthony's primary focus all these years would make you a little wary. But you don't really have to worry about that, you know. You can be quite a little dynamo yourself. I don't know which one of you I'd back if it came to a showdown."

"Thanks for the vote of confidence." She wrinkled her nose at him affectionately. "I wish I could be as sure of my strength as you and Anthony seem to be. He's always telling me how strong and independent I am too. It seems to be some sort of magic incantation around here."

They had arrived at the house now and were climbing the steps to the front door. "That should make you feel more secure if anything would. Do you think that if he values those qualities in you so highly, he'd ever try to crush them?"

"I don't know. How can anyone tell what Anthony will do?" she asked wearily. She couldn't tell him it wasn't his forcefulness she feared so much as her own loving desire that had flared so quickly last night. "That's the whole point. Even after all these years Anthony is still almost a stranger to me. How can you trust a stranger?"

"Think about it," Beau argued softly. "Has he ever done anything to cause you to distrust him? He's scrupulously honest both in business and personal dealings. He's certainly been fantastically generous to you." He opened the door to allow her to precede him. "And to me. Do you know he's never allowed me even to thank him for putting my life back on the right track? No emotional blackmail and no suspicions. He ignores that part of my life as if it didn't exist." He shook his head. "And because it doesn't exist for him anymore, it doesn't exist for me either. That's a pretty generous gift for anyone to give. It was a fairly ugly time for both of us. Curing an alcoholic is hell on wheels for everyone around him."

Dany blinked rapidly to hold back the tears. "But in this case very worthwhile," she said, lightness masking the huskiness of her voice. "You're an extremely special person, Beau Lantry."

For a moment Beau's mocking panache was banished by unusual awkwardness. "Hey!" he said gruffly. "If you think you're going to embarrass me by crying all over me, you can forget it. Look, it's all in the past. I've got my problem licked now. The only reason I even brought it up was I thought it might help you to understand Anthony a little better." He gave an affectionate tug on her ponytail. "You're a sweet, loving lady with everyone but him. Why don't you give him a chance to enter the magic circle? He may need it even more than the rest of us."

Her eyes darkened with pain. "You're wrong, Beau. Anthony doesn't need anyone. He told me so." Her lips trembled as she tried to smile. "And that makes him very dangerous to someone like me. I think I'd be safer to keep my defenses very high and firm."

There was a sudden flicker of surprise and then a dawning comprehension in the warm hazel eyes gazing into her own. His lips pursed in a soundless whistle. "Like that, Dany?"

She nodded. "Like that," she said simply. "I'll work myself into the ground to give him the gold. It's really his, no matter what he says. But after that I'm going to put all the distance I can between us. He may have been a good friend to you, but with very little effort he could probably tear my life to shreds. I'm not about to give him the opportunity if I can help it." She shrugged off her jacket and took her skate bag from him. Her lashes lowered as her tone became brisk. "So I'll maintain my safe and sheltered role as Anthony's protégée and leave his personal life to the Luisas of the world." Lord, it was sheer torture to get those words out, she thought.

"Maybe that would be best," Beau said after a troubled pause. "Friendship I think you can handle, but I'm not sure you wouldn't be right about anything more . . . intimate. He's not an easy man."

"That's putting it conservatively," she said with a wry smile. "Don't worry, Beau, I—"

"I'm sorry to disturb you, Miss Alexander." The butler's voice was punctiliously polite as he appeared at her side. "Mr. Malik has called twice since you've been down at the pond practicing. He was quite surprised you weren't at the rink and couldn't be reached by phone. He asked you to call him at his apartment in New York immediately on your return. The number is on the pad on his desk in the library."

She felt a queer little flutter in the pit of her stomach that was half excitement, half trepidation. "Thank you," she said absently, handing him her skate bag and jacket. "Will you have these taken to my room? I'll make the call right away."

"Certainly." He turned and started to mount the stairs with august dignity.

"Why don't you go lie down and rest for a while?" Beau asked gently. "You can always make the call later. If you like, I'll give him a ring and tell him you'll phone after dinner tonight."

She shook her head. "We both know when Anthony asks someone to call, it's tantamount to a royal decree." She was already striding briskly down the hall toward the library, but she looked over her shoulder to give him a reassuring smile. "Thanks for trying to run interference, Beau, but I'll be fine. I'm a dynamo, remember?"

"How could I forget?" he asked with a graceful mocking bow. "You remind me a bit of Scarlett O'Hara without her more unpleasant qualities. You were never meant to be a Yankee, Dany. It's some ghastly celestial mistake."

"If you say so," she said absently, her thoughts already on the phone call to be made in the next few moments. "I'll see you at dinner, Beau."

As she was listening to the phone ring a little bit later, she didn't feel like anything even remotely resembling a dynamo. She felt miserably unsure, and a barrage of memories of last night's intimacies assaulted her with a force that caused her uneasiness to escalate more by the second. How stupid to be so vulnerable, she thought with an impatience that sent a sudden tingle of defiance surging through her. It came just in time, for the next moment Anthony picked up the receiver with a terse "Malik."

"Anthony?" Her voice was amazingly cool, she congratulated herself. "Dany. I understand you've been trying to get in touch with me."

"What the hell were you doing at the pond?" His voice was roughly impatient. "That snow last night would have made it totally unfit for any serious practice."

"It wasn't all that bad," she said evasively. "I'll work out on the rink tomorrow. Beau said the triples went fairly well."

"And the spins?"

She wasn't about to confess they lacked the needed speed. "Why don't you ask him?" she asked with dulcet sweetness. "Would you like me to put him on?"

"No." His reply was terse. "I'll see them myself tomorrow. Work on your compulsory figures in the morning. I want to go over your long freestyle program with you in the afternoon."

"Yes, master," she said meekly. "It shall be as you decree. And now, if that's all you wanted, I'd like to change for dinner."

"That's not all." There was a long pause. "Paul Jens said you didn't arrive at Briarcliff until nearly three thirty. Pete picked you up at eleven. Where were you all that time?"

Her hand tightened on the receiver. "I stopped in at Jack Kowalt's apartment and had lunch with him." She could sense the crackling tension on the other end of the line but managed to keep her tone calmly confident. "You'll be glad to know that Jack accepted both of our apologies. He's a very understanding man."

"And how understanding was he?" Anthony's voice was silky. "You were there long enough for him to demonstrate in detail just how understanding he could be." His tone dropped to menacing softness. "Perhaps I should have been there when you awoke this morning. Were you wanting a man so badly that you had to run to Kowalt to assuage it?"

"No!" She took a deep breath and tried to regain her composure. "I told you it wasn't like that with us. But even if it were, I wouldn't let you interfere. I'll see Jack whenever I like. I won't have my life choreographed by you."

There was a long silence. "And what about last night?"

She moistened her lips nervously. "Last night was a mistake," she said quickly. She let her breath out shakily. "It wouldn't work out between us, Anthony. I don't want to become an appendage to any man. And with you that's what it would come down to in the end. You're that kind of person."

"Am I?" Anthony's tone was expressionless. "I thought you might have some sort of backlash reaction from last night. I didn't think it would be this radical, however. Not enough to drive you back to Kowalt."

"It's not a backlash," she denied firmly. "I'm just thinking clearly now. You're a very desirable and experienced man, Anthony. And it was perfectly natural that our good judgment was destroyed by a chemistry as potent as ours. But you can see it's better that we continue as we have been all these years."

"The hell I can!" The violence in his tone was so raw, it shocked her. "You may think you're going to be able to turn your back on last night

and walk away, but I'll be damned if I'll let you."
There was a moment's silence in which he was obviously struggling for control. "If I hadn't been so blasted noble, you wouldn't be giving me this damn lecture on the wisdom of maintaining your independence. You'd be here with me now, with your legs wrapped around me while I—"

"Anthony!" She felt a melting heat in her loins, and her exclamation sounded faint and breathless even to her own ears.

"You would; you know it as well as I do." His voice was suddenly unutterably weary. "I won't be such a fool again. Enough is enough. From now on our relationship comes first and to hell with Calgary. I wasn't comfortable in the role of a self-sacrificing Galahad anyway. I'll see you tomorrow, Dany."

Before she could reply, he'd hung up the receiver.

Chapter 4

"Is there some kind of unwritten law that says skaters have to be up at the crack of dawn?" Marta complained with a sleepy yawn. She watched blearily as Dany, before the vanity mirror, pinned her hair up into its customary topknot. "I thought when we came here to Briarcliff, some of the pressure would be off you." She sighed. "I might have known better. You're the one who applies most of the pressure on yourself."

Dany looked over her shoulder with a quick grin. "I do my best concentrating before the sun comes up." She made a face. "I'm going to need every bit of concentration I can muster while I'm working on those compulsory figures. They're definitely not my strong point." She watched Marta straighten up from leaning indolently against the doorjamb to cross her room and drop into the beige Queen Anne chair a few feet away with a flurry of her sheer blue chiffon negligee.

Marta's passion for soft, ultrafeminine lingerie was completely at odds with her pragmatic image and always came as a surprise to Dany. It just went to show that no one was predictable. After Beau's revelation last night she found herself looking at Marta with new eyes. She'd been so involved in her own work, she'd taken everyone around her terribly for granted, she realized now. Just because Marta was maternal and protective with her, it didn't mean that was the face she revealed to the rest of the world. Marta had been divorced for some years before she'd come to work for Anthony, but what did Dany really know about her personal life? Marta was a very private person and seemed to prefer to keep her own counsel regarding her past.

Marta smothered another yawn. "I don't see

why those judges make you do compulsory figures anyway. The free skating is much nicer to watch."

"It's all a part of the sport." Dany stood up and smoothed the skintight aqua-and-white-striped jumpsuit she was wearing. She always preferred a skirt and tights when she skated, liking the way the material flowed around her with every movement. Still, no one could deny that these jumpsuits were warmer. While she was working on the slow precision figures it would be much more practical. "Why don't you go back to bed? I'll be working most of the day and won't need you until late afternoon."

"I just might do that." Marta struggled to her feet and crossed to the closet to pull out Dany's skate bag. "Lord, I hate getting up early. I seem destined to spend most of my life stumbling around with my eyes half closed." She slipped Dany's white leather jacket off the hanger. "First on that farm in Minnesota where I grew up, then in the Army, and now with a workaholic skater who doesn't have the sense to know every day should start at noon."

"Sorry." An amused smile tugged at Dany's lips

as she took the jacket and skate bag Marta handed her. "I guess it's the nature of the beast." Her dark eyes twinkled. "Of course, since you can't seem to convince me of that, you could join me instead. I've never seen you on skates, Marta. Why don't you come down to the rink and we'll do some freestyle warm-ups before I start to practice?"

"Me?" Marta's blue eyes widened in shock. "You've got to be kidding!" She shook her head firmly. "I don't skate."

"Then I'll teach you," Dany coaxed. "Come on, Marta, you'll love it once you start."

"Oh, no, I won't." Marta scowled. "I had lessons once, but it took me only a very short time to realize I'd never be a skater." She paused before adding reluctantly, "There's something physically wrong with me. I'll never be able to skate."

"Physically?" Dany asked with quick concern. "I didn't know. What is it?" Marta appeared to be in the most robust health. Perhaps it was only weak ankles. A great many people were afflicted with that.

"I can only skate backward," Marta answered

glumly. "There's got to be something wrong with my equilibrium. Every time I skate forward, I fall on my tush. Skating backward, I'm Peggy Fleming. Skating forward, I'm Bozo the Clown."

Dany was trying desperately to keep a straight face. "I'm sure with practice—"

"I *did* practice," Marta said indignantly. "I tell you, there's something wrong with the way I'm put together." She looked speculatively down at her ample bosom. "Maybe I just kind of overbalance."

Dany was chuckling helplessly now. "Why didn't you keep on skating anyway? A reverse Peggy Fleming isn't half bad."

"Oh yeah? You just try it sometime. It gets lonely as hell skating backward all the time when everyone else is skating forward. It's all very well to march to the tune of a different drummer but skating to one is an entirely different cup of tea!"

Dany shook her head, still chuckling. "I can see your point," she said solemnly. She leaned forward and gave Marta an affectionate kiss on the cheek. "If you change your mind, the offer is always open. Between Beau and me, we should be able to get you on the right track. We'll look upon it as the supreme challenge to our expertise."

"Maybe someday," Marta said with a good deal of skepticism. She frowned suddenly. "I don't suppose you're intending to eat any breakfast before you start working? You look like a puff of wind would blow you away in that jumpsuit. You didn't eat more than a few bites at dinner last night."

Dany quickly lowered her eyes as she turned to leave. She had been in such emotional turmoil last night after the phone call from Anthony, she'd barely been conscious of eating at all. "Beau will see that I stop to eat breakfast sometime this morning," she said vaguely. "He's as much of a mother hen as you are about my losing weight."

"That's because Anthony's on his tail if he notices even an ounce difference," Marta said grimly. "Even when he's halfway across the country, he hears about it. It's not exactly pleasant to be on the receiving end when Anthony's not pleased about something."

She was well aware of that, Dany thought wearily as she opened the door. Following last night's confrontation she hadn't been able to sleep until the wee hours of the morning, and then only for a restless few hours.

Luisa Kendall was absolutely gorgeous as usual. Her knee-length raccoon poncho was worn with her customary dash over designer jeans tucked into brown knee-length boots. Her long, dark hair was tumbling about her shoulders in stylish profusion, and her violet eyes, framed in long lashes that made them appear even larger, were sparkling with good nature as she waved at Dany from behind the barricade that surrounded the rink.

"Hi, Dany," she called as she leaned her elbows on the balustrade. "I love your outfit. You look like a *très chic* skin diver or something."

"How would you know?" Anthony asked, an indulgent smile curving his lips. "The closest you've ever come to any kind of aquatic undertaking is dipping your toes in the water to wash the sand off."

Dany stopped in the middle of the figure she'd been tracing and with a bright smile carefully masked the shock she was experiencing. She suddenly felt very naked and exposed alone out on the ice in the middle of the rink. Luisa's appearance at Briarcliff with Anthony had come as a complete surprise and caught her off guard. After the remarks he'd made on the phone, the last thing she'd expected was to have him show up with his mistress in tow or to have him stand there gazing at her with cool detachment as if nothing had changed. Well, perhaps nothing *had* changed. Perhaps he'd thought over what she'd said and decided it made sense to go along with her way of thinking. Luisa's appearance here certainly seemed to indicate that, Dany thought, simultaneously feeling an irrational burst of pain.

"Thanks, Luisa," she called back. "But it's not supposed to be fashionable, just functional. It's specially insulated to keep out the cold."

"Whatever." Luisa shrugged her elegantly furred shoulders. "It's still pretty, and that's the bottom line."

At least it was for Luisa, Dany thought as she skated over to the bench behind the balustrade that was across the rink from where they were standing. Luisa loved pretty clothes with a passion. That was one of the reasons she'd chosen to become a photographer's model. She was very successful at it, too, when she made the effort. Unfortunately most aspects of her career were too much effort for Luisa's good-natured but indolent temperament. Not that she needed to work, Dany thought as she started to unlace her skates with feverish swiftness. Anthony, for over a year now, had kept her very well supplied with every luxury. An undemanding beauty like Luisa was exactly what he wanted in a mistress.

"Those skates are different from the other ones you usually wear, aren't they?" Luisa's eyes were bright with curiosity. She'd wandered around the rink and was standing by the bench. Beau and Anthony were still across the rink absorbed in discussion, and Luisa had no doubt become bored and was seeking distraction.

Dany nodded. "The blades have a wider radius. I use them only for compulsory figures. They make a clearer tracing for the judges."

"I like the dancing better," Luisa said. "That looks like you're having a real ball." Her eyes went around the large rink, lingering on the arched, paneled skylight that covered most of the ceiling. "This is really very nice. Anthony says it's relatively new, compared to the rest of the estate."

"Anthony had it built about nine years ago," Dany said quietly. "He said it would be more convenient for practice."

"I can see that." A puzzled frown suddenly knotted Luisa's brow. "But you've not been here for almost six years, I understand."

"That's right," she answered briefly. Most of the time she liked Luisa, but she was finding that eager curiosity a little hard to take today. "Is this the first time you've been to Briarcliff?"

The other woman nodded her fashionably tousled head. "I've been to Anthony's apartment in town, naturally, but he's never brought me here." Long, dark hair spread over gray silk pillows. Why did the thought twist inside her like a knife? "It really surprised me last night when he asked me to come up here for a few days."

Last night. He'd been with Luisa last night, she thought dully. He'd probably gone straight from talking to her to Luisa's very willing arms.

"You're staying overnight?" Well, why shouldn't she? Briarcliff was Anthony's to do with as he wished now. She had no right to resent any of his choice of guests. But she did, dammit. She *did*.

"Anthony thought I might find it entertaining." Luisa made a face. "I don't want to hurt your feelings, but I can't say I'm looking forward to it. I'm a city girl to begin with, and I can take just so much of this ice skating. It makes me tired just watching you." She grinned appealingly. "No offense."

"None taken," Dany said lightly as she finished tying the laces of her tennis shoes. "Unless you're involved, the mechanics can get pretty boring."

"I'd think it would be easy to get involved with a coach like Beau." Luisa's eyes narrowed on Beau's trim, powerful body and lean, good-looking face. "It must be very interesting being on the road with a hunk like that."

"Beau?" Dany's lips twisted in a grin. "You've got to be joking. I'm strictly business with our Confederate Don Juan. He's got two or three lovely ladies in every city we visit."

"So I've heard," Luisa said lightly. "I can't say

that I blame them. I've always been a pushover for a wicked, golden-eyed devil."

"Wicked?" Dany's eyes widened. "We can't be talking about the same man. There's nothing wicked about Beau."

"No?" A quizzical smile tugged at Luisa's lips. "That's not what I hear from his discarded mistresses. Not that they were complaining, you understand. In fact, they'd have been very disappointed if he hadn't lived up to their expectations." Luisa unconsciously moistened her lips, narrowing her gaze on Beau's face. "He's reputed to be very generous with his farewell presents as well. How does it feel to have one of the richest men in America at your beck and call?"

"I never thought about it," Dany said uncomfortably. She'd heard vague stories, of course, about Beau's background. Everyone in the United States knew about the Lantry Trust and the orphaned heir who'd been the focus of any number of custody suits during his childhood. "And he's not at my beck and call. We work together."

"Still, it's odd he'd take on a subservient position." Luisa's face was speculative. "Rumor has it that he's not a man to accept any kind of restraint meekly. I don't suppose he has an unrequited passion for you or something like that?"

Dany's glance followed hers to the man who'd been her anchor and security in a constantly changing world for the last six years. She tried to understand how anyone could see Beau as the devilish charmer of Luisa's description. Yes, there *was* sensuality and a little recklessness to the cut of his lips, and, now that she thought about it, there had been moments when there'd been a wild, untamed glint in those gold-flecked eyes. She shook her head as if to clear it. No, Luisa had to be wrong. "Then the rumors are definitely in error," she said firmly. "Beau's one of the steadiest, most reliable men I've ever met, and we're only very good friends."

"Pity." Luisa grinned. "An affair with your coach wouldn't only be fun, it'd be very convenient. You know how I always favor the easiest way."

Yes, Dany knew that. Luisa would always take exactly what Anthony wanted to give her and never ask for more. It was no doubt a very satisfying relationship for both of them. She jumped lightly to her feet and smiled with an effort. "Beau and I are going to have a sandwich and soup for lunch before we begin working again. There's a lounge and kitchenette in the back of the rink. Would you and Anthony like to join us?"

"No, thanks." Luisa raised her chin in mock hauteur. "I'm not about to mingle with the hoi polloi. Anthony's promised me a gourmet luncheon at the main house as my reward for journeying to the wilds of Connecticut. He said he'd recently hired a cook who was utterly superb. Is he really that good or have I been had?"

"What?" Dany tried desperately to remember the quality of the dinner she'd scarcely tasted last night. "Oh, I'm sure you'll enjoy it very much," she said vaguely as she turned to leave. "Will you be coming back here after lunch?"

"And watch two sexy men give all their attention to another woman?" Luisa shook her head. "I'm too vain for that kind of punishment. I'll settle in and find a good book to read in front of the fire. I'll see you at dinner."

"Right." Dany waved casually and set off briskly

for the lounge, keeping her gaze turned studiously away from the two men across the rink. She wasn't ready to meet those glacier-green eyes. She was still too shocked and raw from that first encounter.

She purposely blocked everything from her mind as she opened a can of bean and bacon soup, poured it into a saucepan, and put it on one of the burners of the stove. She was placing two ham-and-cheese sandwiches in the microwave oven to heat when Beau walked into the kitchenette. His hazel eyes were concerned. "Okay?" he asked quietly.

"You tell me," she said, purposely misunderstanding him. "Did you get a chance to check those last tracings?"

He shook his head. "Anthony was too busy cross-examining me about your training sessions yesterday and today. The earlier ones looked fine though." He paused. "Anthony wants you to go over your long routine for him this afternoon. Are you up to it?"

"Of course, I'm up to it," she said, her tone brittle. Oh, what was the use? Dany told herself. She abruptly dropped the facade. "Will you please stop looking at me as if you expected me to fall into a Victorian swoon? So what if Anthony's brought Luisa with him today? It's happened before, and it will probably happen again. I'm not about to let it affect my work." She turned and took the saucepan from the burner. "After all, nothing's really changed." God, she wished that were true. She'd give anything if she could have turned back time and never known that night in Anthony's apartment.

"If you say so," Beau said slowly.

"I say so," she answered firmly. "Now sit down and I'll dish up the soup. It may not be the gourmet delight Luisa and Anthony are probably enjoying, but it's hot. That's enough for me after five hours on the ice."

The afternoon proved easier than she'd expected, largely due to the fact that Anthony exhibited a cool professionalism that she could respond to with equal composure. He didn't bother to put on his skates, but sat on one of the spectator chairs in the two tiers that surrounded the rink and quietly watched while Beau put her through her paces. Occasionally he'd have her do something over or call out to Beau to keep an eye out for a slight flaw in style or technique. For the most part, however, he merely sat and watched, his eyes narrowed and thoughtful as he had her go over the freestyle program repeatedly until she was so tired, she could feel her muscles ache, then go numb with weariness. Once or twice she noticed a worried frown darken Beau's face near the end of the grueling session, and she knew he would have protested if she hadn't given him a fierce glance and shaken her head at him.

There was nothing vindictive in Anthony's drive for perfection. He simply didn't understand half-way measures and would have driven himself just as relentlessly to the point of exhaustion. In an odd way she was proud she had the stamina to keep up with his demands and that he had the confidence she could meet any test he set for her.

The last long rays of late afternoon were streaming through the skylight when he finally terminated the session and called Beau and Dany over to give them the rest of the notes he'd made on the afternoon's workout. He hadn't missed a thing;

his criticism was incisive and all-encompassing. But for every criticism, he offered a suggestion on its correction. At the end of the list he sat back in his chair. "But those are all little things," he said, his expression suddenly grave. "What we've got to work on is the real reason you lost the championship, Dany. I think I've got a handle on that now. You're not getting into the ice. There's no affinity there. It's an ephemeral element, but the judges will notice it every time. An ice skater has got to look as if she belongs out there, as if she belongs to the ice itself. If she doesn't, it plays hell with her style."

"I know that," Dany said, brushing a loose tendril of hair away from her face. "You've told me often enough." She tried to smile. "I'll work on it."

He shook his head. "I think that may be the problem." His eyes were thoughtful. "It may be that you're overtraining. You're working so hard, you're losing that fine edge. Perhaps it would be better to ease up a little."

"Ease up?" He couldn't be serious! With the Olympics less than a month away? "For heaven's sake, you've just given me a list a mile long of all the things I'm doing wrong and then tell me to take it easy?" She shook her head incredulously. "You know I can't do that."

His lips tightened. "I also know that your figures in the compulsories will probably leave a lot to be desired. You always get a little impatient and it's reflected in your scores. You're going to have to make up those points on the freestyle, and you can't do it if you don't get into the ice." He stood up, his hands jammed in the pockets of his sheepskin jacket. "You've come a long way to get to Calgary, Dany. I'm not about to let you blow it now."

"I won't blow it," she said hotly. "But I won't sit around and fiddle while Rome burns either. I have to work, dammit."

"You *will* work." Anthony turned away, his face implacable. "But you won't overtrain. Make up your mind to that, Dany." Before she could speak he was walking rapidly away.

"Damn!" She drew a deep breath and her fists clenched in frustration. "He doesn't understand, Beau. I still have so far to go, so much to perfect. I can't relax now."

"He may be right, you know," Beau said, considering. "He usually is when it comes to skating. I've been conscious of something being wrong lately, but I haven't been able to put my finger on it. You just may have lost the edge. Perhaps we'd better rethink your training regimen for the next few weeks."

"No!" Her cry had an element of desperation in it. She needed to work, to concentrate on something other than the turbulent emotional state Anthony had thrown her into. She deliberately released her clenched fists and tried to speak with calm persuasion. "He's wrong, Beau. You know I'd be a nervous wreck if I didn't have enough work to keep me busy. We'll keep on just as we have been."

His expression was troubled. "We'll have to see, sugar. Anthony seemed pretty determined." He shrugged. "Well, we'll worry about it tomorrow. Now I'd better deliver you back to Marta for a massage or you'll never make it to dinner. That was quite a workout today."

She felt her tension relax as it always did in Beau's soothing presence. "Worry about it tomorrow?" she teased. "Now who's sounding like Scarlett O'Hara?"

"I told you I admired the lady," he said with a lazy grin. "There weren't many characters I could feel an affinity with in *Gone With the Wind*. Ashley Wilkes was too much of a namby-pamby for my taste, and Rhett Butler was a Yankee. That doesn't leave much for a virile, dashing rebel like me." He took her elbow and pushed her gently toward the door. "You know you can tap that priceless store of southern gallantry at any time, Dany. All you have to do is say the word, and I'll make your excuses at dinner tonight. You sure don't need any emotional upsets after that physical marathon you went through today."

"There won't be any emotional upsets," she said steadily, her shoulders unconsciously squaring. "None at all."

Her shoulders remained squared and her jaw set all that evening as she tried to conduct herself with a cool, mature poise that revealed nothing of the constant pain that was tearing her apart. She had no right to resent the attention Anthony was lavishing on Luisa, nor the casual intimacy they both displayed in every word and movement. It had been her choice, and she should be strong enough to subdue the anger and resentment. She *was* strong enough. She'd be damned if she'd let Anthony see how his charming little double entendres to Luisa were affecting her.

She plastered a bright smile on her face and proceeded to be very vivacious and charming. That gaiety was generously reinforced by several glasses of wine at the table and two more in the drawing room after dinner that she was barely conscious of drinking. She was aware only of how ravishing Luisa looked in a sapphire gown that showed so much cleavage, Beau had nearly choked on his own ginger ale when he'd first caught sight of her. Anthony's admiration hadn't been so obvious, but why should it be? she thought miserably. He was accustomed to all of Luisa's charms, both clothed and unclothed. He'd probably be taking that gown off her soon in the privacy of his suite with the same deft deliberation he'd demonstrated to Dany so recently.

The thought pierced her cool aplomb like a fiery arrow, and suddenly she couldn't take any more. She murmured an apology and something about needing an early night. She practically ran from the room, conscious of Luisa's expression of surprise, Beau's concern, and Anthony's lack of any expression at all. Oh, Lord, had she given herself away? Surely not. She'd been in firm control until the very end.

Her head was whirling dizzily, and she felt suddenly unsteady on her feet. Oh, no, was she tipsy? That's all she needed to make this disaster of an evening complete. She tried to remember how many drinks she'd had, but it was all a blur of sapphire chiffon and glacier-green eyes. One thing was certain: She'd never be able to make it upstairs until she got over this dizziness.

She moved with slow, careful methodicalness toward the library. She found if she took one step at a time, the hall didn't shimmy quite so badly. When the door closed behind her, she leaned against it with a sigh of relief. In a few minutes she'd make it to that huge leather chair by the desk that beckoned so invitingly, and just stay here until she felt better. *How stupid could you get?* she thought with disgust. She never drank more than a couple of glasses of wine, even on social occasions, and she had to pick tonight of all nights to exceed that moderation. She was lucky she hadn't made a complete fool of herself. She probably would have if she hadn't been so tense and wary; the liquor hadn't really hit her until she'd relaxed her guard.

There, she'd reached the chair and it hadn't been nearly so difficult as she thought it would be. She sank into its cushiony depths, vaguely conscious of the scent of leather and the crackle of the logs in the fireplace across the room. It was very pleasant here in this dim, cozy room, she thought vaguely. And if the rich colors of Anthony's new kilim carpet would stop blurring and running together, she'd be quite content. Anthony. She mustn't think about Anthony or sapphire gowns or anything but making the room regain its equilibrium. She'd just close her eyes for a moment and everything would soon be back in clear focus. She was sure of it. All she had to do was close her eyes for a moment. . . .

"Dany."

It was Anthony's voice and she tensed. Then she relaxed as she realized she must be imagining it. Anthony couldn't be here. He was with Luisa, helping her out of that blue siren's gown. Besides, Anthony's voice was hard and incisive, not velvet-deep with tenderness.

"Wake up, Dany."

She *was* awake, couldn't he see that? Well, perhaps he couldn't. Somehow she'd forgotten to open her eyes. No wonder; the lids were terribly heavy when she did open them a second later. But it was well worth the effort. Anthony was kneeling by the chair, and he was so beautiful. He'd shed his evening jacket and tie; his white dress shirt was unbuttoned and revealed the strong bronze column of his throat. His hair was dark satin in the firelight, and his eyes were rich and glowing with the same tenderness that had been in his voice.

"You're not supposed to be here," she whispered solemnly, her dark eyes enormous in her thin, pale face.

"I'm not?" His lips twitched slightly. "Just where am I supposed to be?"

Her eyes filled with tears. "Helping Luisa out of her gown. Why aren't you doing it?"

He picked up her hand on the arm of the chair and lifted the palm up to his lips. "Luisa doesn't require a lady's maid." His lips brushed her skin gently. "And I had an idea you might. I was a little worried about you, so I went to your room before I turned in. Then I had to make a room-to-room search before I located you."

"You shouldn't have left Luisa so long," she said gloomily. "She'll miss you."

"Will she? I don't think so." He was just holding her hand now with an affectionate surety that was marvelously comforting. "She's proved to be very understanding in our relationship to date."

"That's because she's a very nice woman." She glared at him accusingly. "All of your mistresses have been nice."

"Is that some kind of crime?" His eyes were twinkling. "I enjoy being around nice women. Bitchiness has never appealed to me."

"No. It's just that they'd have been easier to

take if they'd been perfect shrews." Oh, Lord, why was she saying all this? It was as if all her barriers and safeguards had been banished, or rather, as if they weren't necessary anymore. There was no threat in Anthony holding her hands so gently and gazing at her with eyes that were both tender and amused. "Oh, dear. I *am* tipsy, aren't I?"

"Perhaps a little." He cocked his head, considering. "You drank a little more than you usually do, and you were pretty well zonked from exhaustion from your workout even before dinner began."

It was nice of him to make excuses for her, but she might as well make a complete confession. "I'd never be able to walk a straight line," she told him gravely. "I barely made it to this chair."

"Don't worry about it," he said easily. "When you're ready to go to bed, I'll carry you up. Okay?"

It sounded wonderful and she nodded happily. Then her face darkened in a frown. "Luisa . . . ?"

". . . is safely tucked in bed and snoozing away," he said, his hand tightening on hers. "Not in *my* bed, I might add. Not anymore. There won't be any woman but you in my bed from now on. I knew that the day you came back to Briarcliff."

"You could have told me," she complained indignantly. Her eyes filled with tears again. "You never tell me anything!"

"I think you're a little more tipsy than I thought." A little smile tugged at his lips. Such a beautiful, sensual smile, Dany mused. "If you recall, you've been so wary of me, you were ready to kick me out of your life last night." He was playing absently with her fingers. "Maybe I was a bit afraid of you, too, or I wouldn't have brought Luisa here today. It could have been an unconscious defense mechanism."

"Afraid of me!"

He nodded. "You mean too much to me," he said simply, his eyes meeting hers with a vulnerability that brought an ache to her throat. "You're the only person in the whole damn world who could hurt me. That frightens me, Dany." He drew a deep breath. "I told myself that I brought Luisa here to shake you up a little, to make you see how much it would hurt to put anyone between us." He lifted her hand and held it to his cheek. "And it did hurt, didn't it, love? It hurt me when I thought about you with Kowalt, but I couldn't stand seeing you suffer the same kind of torment I'd gone through." He was rubbing her palm over the broad, hard contour of his cheekbone. "No more barriers between us, okay? No game playing, no wariness, just honesty." He smiled with an effort. "That may be even more difficult for me than you."

It probably would be, she thought dreamily, for suddenly the fear that had been a predominant element in her love for Anthony for so long was completely gone. It had been banished by his confession of vulnerability, drowned in a protectiveness that was almost fiercely maternal. It was strange how buoyant and free she felt without that albatross dragging at her. How strong. As if for the first time in her life she could meet Anthony on his own ground.

"You know, I'm glad I'm tipsy," she said huskily. "It makes all the hard, cutting edges beautifully blurred and the complicated things so clear." Her fingertips feathered lightly across the plane of his cheek to his lips. "I know you don't approve of weakness, but just this time I'm glad I fell from grace."

He frowned. "You make me sound like a pompous ass. Everyone has weaknesses, me most of all. I sure as hell can't judge other people's faults when I have so many of my own. I just think everyone should fight them." He gave her hand an affectionate squeeze before releasing it and standing up. "Come on, I'd better get you to bed. You're in no shape for any meaningful discussions tonight."

He was wrong, she thought vaguely as he gathered her up in his arms and strode swiftly toward the door. If she hadn't been in this strange golden state of limbo, she'd never have been able to banish the fear that had crippled her emotionally for so long. Now the way was clear for understanding and growth. She tried to tell him that, but the words were difficult to form when she was so deliciously warm and content in his arms, so she settled for protesting. "I don't want to go to bed."

"You just think you don't." He was climbing the gracefully curving stairway with lithe strength. "You'll be out like a light in a few minutes."

"Rhett Butler."

He looked down at her, his brow arched inquiringly. "What?"

"Rhett Butler carried Scarlett O'Hara up a staircase like this," she said, nestling closer. "Beau doesn't like Rhett. He was a Yankee, you know."

"So I've heard."

"He likes you though," she assured him solemnly. He was very fit, she thought idly. His heart beneath her ear had barely increased its pace during the climb up the stairs. "He's very grateful to you."

His arms tensed around her. "I gather he told you about his problem. He has nothing to be grateful to me for." His voice was suddenly harsh. "I wish to hell he hadn't said anything. I don't want gratitude now or ever. Not from him and not from you. I do what I want to do and nobody owes me anything."

There would have been a time when that harshness might have intimidated her, but that time was past. "All right, nobody owes you anything," she said agreeably. "I'll have to remember that next time I'm tempted to tell you to go to hell when you're playing Simon Legree."

There was a moment of silence and then Anthony's surprised chuckle. "You do that." His lips lightly brushed the top of her head. "Not that it will do you any good. You'll still do things my way."

"We'll see," she said serenely. "You just might get a surprise."

He paused just inside her bedroom door to gaze down at her with a curious mixture of speculation and pride. "I might at that." He kicked the door shut, then made his way carefully across the dark bedroom to the canopy bed in the center of the room. He laid her on the delicate beige paisley counterpane. "As you said, we'll just have to see." He reached out to switch on the lamp on the bedside table. "Tonight, though, I think we'll just concentrate on getting you out of that gown and into bed. Can you sit up?"

"Of course." She proceeded to show him and was immediately punished by a dizziness that forced her to shut her eyes tightly to prevent the

floor from heaving like an unruly sea. Anthony
was immediately sitting beside her on the bed and
she clutched tightly at his shoulders. "With a little
help from my friends," she amended faintly.

"Do you know that's the first time you've ever
called me your friend?" he asked with a thread of
huskiness in his voice. "It's very . . ." He cleared
his throat and spoke with gruff briskness. "I think
you'd better submerge that independence tem-
porarily and let me do it all."

"If you like." She opened her eyes cautiously
and found to her relief the floor had settled into a
solid again.

"I like," Anthony said firmly. His fingers were
unzipping the fastening at the back of the tulle
gown. "This is very pretty. I like you in that shade
of antique gold. It always brings out all the color
in your hair."

"I thought it was beautiful, too, until I saw
Luisa's." She looked up at him with a scowl. "Did
you buy her that gown?"

"Probably. I don't remember," he said casually
as he carefully supported her with one arm while
he pulled the gown down to her waist and then

eased it over her hips. "And I'll give her a generous check so she can buy as many pretty dresses as her heart desires for the next year. By that time she'll have found someone else to pay the bills."

"Won't she be hurt?" Dany's eyes were troubled. "I like Luisa."

"I know you do." His expression softened as he glanced at her face. "Do you think I'd have let her come to your home if I didn't know that?"

"*My* home?" Her eyes widened. "Briarcliff is your home, Anthony. You can bring anyone you like here."

He looked away uneasily and quickly busied himself with pulling off her high-heeled sandals and slipping her beneath the covers. "No, it isn't," he said haltingly. "When I sent you away six years ago, I deeded Briarcliff over to you. Competitive skating isn't the most secure career in the world. I wanted you to have something to fall back on." He scowled fiercely. "It should have been yours anyway, so don't give me any of that gratitude crap."

"No, I won't give you that." She swiftly closed her eyes so he wouldn't see the brightness of unshed tears in their depths. What a wonderful thing to do. "Something to fall back on." Perhaps. But it was her home and she loved it. Even if he wouldn't admit it, that was the real reason he'd given it to her, and that knowledge filled her with a glowing exhilaration that was pure joy. One day soon she'd tell him how she felt, but not now. If she said anything now, he'd mistake it for that cloying gratitude he seemed to despise so much. She opened her eyes, her gaze running lovingly over the bold planes of his still-frowning face. "Well, in that case," she said with mock sternness, "I'd appreciate it if you'd keep your mistresses away from *my* house."

"Yes, ma'am," Anthony said, a smile tugging at his lips. "I'll keep that in mind." He stood up. "We'll discuss any further restrictions you wish to put on your humble tenant in the morning. Good night, Dany."

Her eyes widened in dismay. "You're leaving? I thought you were going to sleep with me."

He stiffened and his grin faded. "I'm not taking Briarcliff out in trade either, Dany. Gratitude is bad enough, but—"

"Oh, for Pete's sake," she said wearily. "I

wasn't suggesting any such thing. I just thought it would be nice if you could hold me and make the world stop going around." Her lips trembled slightly. "You did it before."

"Once was enough for a lifetime," he said, his lips tightening grimly. "I'd never last another night like that one, and there's no way I'm going to take advantage of you while you're under the influence." He hesitated. "You really want me to stay?"

She nodded. "But not if it's going to be difficult for you."

"It's going to be difficult." He sighed. "But not as difficult as lying in another room worrying about you all night." He was dragging the Queen Anne chair from across the room to the bed. He dropped into the chair and reached for her hand, enclosing it with sure, warm strength in his own. "A compromise. Satisfied?"

"Satisfied." She smiled happily. Then she felt a guilty qualm. "You're going to be terribly uncomfortable if you stay there all night. You can leave right after I've gone to sleep."

"Thank you," he said wryly. "I'll keep that in

mind. Now, close your eyes and go to sleep." He reached out and turned off the lamp so that the only light was the moonlight streaming through the dimity curtains at the window across the room. He was only a dim shadow now but his hand holding hers was warm and strong and blessedly secure. She closed her eyes and felt drowsiness flow over her in a soothing tide.

He felt her hand relax under his and knew she was asleep. He also knew there was no question of his leaving her as she'd suggested. Not now. Not when she'd asked him to stay beside her for the first time in her life. It was too precious a victory to yield for mere comfort's sake.

His thumb gently rubbed the palm of her hand. Such small, well-shaped hands, and so graceful, Anthony thought. He loved to watch every eager gesture and movement she made with them. He leaned back in the chair, a reminiscing smile curving his lips. Once, when she'd been about eleven or twelve, he'd been coaching her in a laid-back spin. He'd watched her perform the movement with all the exquisitely graceful, balletic overhead arm-and-hand movements the spin required.

There had been such a look of dreamy exultation on her face that he'd impulsively asked what she'd been thinking of.

"I was pretending I was reaching up to gather stars from the sky," she'd said simply. Then the exultation had faded from her face, and she'd given him that half-apprehensive glance he was accustomed to seeing. "Pretty silly, huh?" she'd murmured. And skated away.

Dany was always reaching for the stars, Anthony thought. Searching and working for the very best in herself and everyone around her. Perhaps he loved that facet of her personality most of all. She would be reaching for one of the brightest stars of all in a few weeks, and he wished to heaven he could wrest it from the firmament for her. God, he wished that!

Well, he couldn't do it. Dany had to fight her own battles, to gather her own stars . . . just as he had. If he tried to interfere, he'd be cheating her in the worst possible way. All he could do was stand aside and watch her struggle, hold her hand like this when she'd let him, and love her. Oh, yes, he could love her.

His head settled against the high back of the chair as he prepared to wait the long hours until dawn. His thoughtful gaze was fastened on Dany's shadowy profile, and his grasp tightened protectively on the hand of the woman who tried to gather stars.

Chapter 5

Anthony wasn't there when she awoke, nor was there any note like the terse one that had met her that morning two days before. It didn't disturb her. This morning she didn't think anything could have disturbed the serenity and sheer joyous exuberance she was feeling. It was much later than she usually rose, almost nine o'clock, and she hurriedly showered, dressed in practice clothes, and ran lightly down the stairs within thirty minutes.

She was met at the bottom of the stairs by Beau, who took one look at her glowing face and sparkling eyes and lifted a quizzical brow. "I thought you'd be dragging this morning," he said. "Bags under the eyes and groaning with every cautious step. You're not used to the sauce you were swilling last night."

"What a disgusting expression." She made a face at him. "I did *not* swill. I sipped delicately and with great style."

"If a trifle copiously."

She nodded ruefully. "Definitely copiously. Oh, well, no harm done. I have a trace of a headache, but I'll be rid of that once I've started to practice." She checked the leather-banded watch on her wrist. "I'll have some toast and coffee and be with you in ten minutes. Okay?"

"Uh-uh." Beau shook his bronze head. "No way, sugar. I received detailed instructions from Anthony before he left about the schedule you're to follow today." He grimaced. "You're not going to like it."

"Left?" she asked. "Anthony's not here?"

Beau nodded. "He left about forty-five minutes ago with the luscious Luisa. She took her bags. Evidently she's not planning on coming back."

"I'm sorry. I didn't say good-bye," she murmured absently. Somehow she hadn't thought Anthony would leave without speaking to her. For a moment it cast a shadow over her soaring spirits, but only for a moment. Then she gave herself an admonishing shake. What had she expected, for heaven's sake? Last night had been only the beginning. They'd laid the groundwork for a new kind of relationship, but that was all. They had a long way to go. Anthony was still as enigmatic and complex as he'd ever been. It was only her attitude that had changed. But that was enough. She'd make it enough. "Did he leave any message for me?"

"Several," Beau drawled. "First, you're to have a long, leisurely breakfast. I'm to see that you eat properly, upon threat of mutilation. Second, you're to be permitted three uplifting hours on the ice doing compulsory figures." She scowled. "I thought that would hurt."

"I worked on those yesterday," she objected.

"Anthony says you're to do them today too. Then you may rest, have a light lunch, and, if you feel like it, you can work on ballet at the barre for a while before dinner."

"Three hours on the ice and just on the figures." She shook her head. "I can't do that. What can Anthony be thinking?"

He shrugged. "He asked that you meet him at ten o'clock tonight at the rink, so he may plan on going over the long program with you himself."

She felt her heart leap. "Anthony's coming back today?"

Beau nodded, his gaze narrowed on her face that was suddenly alight. "He was expecting to be at Dynathe until early evening, but he said to tell you he'd be back by ten at the latest. He's having to squeeze your training in between board meetings."

"I suppose I should be honored," she said lightly. "I'd better be sure to get plenty of rest today so I'll be fresh when he gets around to me."

"You're not as upset as I thought you'd be," Beau said, his face thoughtful. "No arguments?"

"Not at the moment," she said with a serene smile as she tucked her arm into his. "But as your

Scarlett pointed out, tomorrow is another day. Now suppose you escort me into the breakfast room and start this force-feeding process Anthony's so set upon."

There were no lights streaming from the tall arched windows of the gray stone building that housed the rink as she walked swiftly up the path, and for a moment she felt a stab of disappointment. He hadn't been able to make it back to Briarcliff after all, then. She shouldn't have expected it, she supposed. Anthony was a terribly busy man, and it was perfectly natural that he should become so involved, he would forget even to call and tell her he couldn't return as planned. Her mind made all the appropriate excuses, but it didn't help lift the crushing weight of depression that was suddenly bearing down upon her.

It wasn't until she opened the door that she heard it: the triumphant strains of Ravel's "Bolero" soaring through the empty rink with the fiery glory of an army with pennants flying. No, not quite empty, she realized with a swift surge of excitement.

Anthony was in the center of the ice, dressed in a black crew-neck sweater and black jeans. She had a fleeting memory of the first time she'd seen him so long ago. A dark flame, she'd thought him then, and he hadn't really changed much in the years since. He was attacking the ice with the same incredible grace that was pure breathtaking beauty to watch. A triple executed with absolute precision, a spin that was a blur of high-speed motion, a camel that was sheer poetry.

As she'd noticed, he hadn't turned on any of the lights, but she could still see him with daylight clarity. The moon's rays were streaming through the skylight that covered most of the ceiling and cast a silver glow over the glittering ice and the man who was making it his own.

She softly closed the door and slowly made her way across the arena to the bench beside the sound unit in the shadows at the rim of the rink, not taking her eyes off Anthony's lithe figure. He hadn't seen her yet, and she wanted to take advantage of this rare opportunity to watch unobserved as Anthony released all the passionate intensity he usually kept leashed. She sat down on the bench, automatically unzipped her skate case, drew out her skates, and slipped them on. Lord, the height of that split was fantastic. There was no question that Anthony was getting into the ice, she thought ruefully as she swiftly laced up her skates. Even in that split when he'd left the ice to soar, the observer had confidence it would receive him like an eager lover when he returned to it.

As she would receive him if he came to her. That sudden realization came as no real surprise. The tingle of breathless anticipation she'd attempted to smother all day, the way she'd dressed tonight with instinctive ritual, the sense of dreamlike inevitability she was experiencing now. She hadn't come to practice. She wanted to belong to Anthony, and she'd come to him to offer herself with the primitive simplicity of woman.

But how was she going to make certain that Anthony would accept her offer? He'd almost driven them both crazy the other night with his maddening scruples about waiting until after Calgary, and last night he'd been just as self-disciplined. Well, she had no use for self-discipline at the moment, and she'd just have to make sure Anthony didn't either. The first item on the agenda was to change that music. Anthony was magnificent as a solo performer, but right now she was more interested in a duet.

Anthony stopped in midmovement when she removed the "Bolero" tape and inserted her own Olympic program cassette. The hauntingly beautiful strains of "Somewhere in Time" began to weave their poignant spell. His eyes searched the shadows by the bench. "Dany?"

"Yes," she answered, trying to steady the quiver of excitement in her voice. She skated toward him out of the dark. "You're a very private person, Anthony. It's not often I get a chance to watch you work out. I've been here for some time."

"I thought you might be," he said to her surprise. She stopped a few feet from him, where she could see the silver-green of his eyes in the shadowy darkness of his face. "And I'm not always that reserved. There are times when every male of the species wants to spread his plumage and strut a bit." He paused. "The time of courtship."

She felt the breath leave her body. "And were you strutting for me?"

"I was doing my damnedest. Did I please you, Dany?"

"Oh, yes, you pleased me." She laughed shakily. "You pleased me very much." Her hands flipped the pleats of her skating skirt. "I think perhaps I wanted to strut a little myself tonight. Do *I* please you?"

His gaze ran over her with lingering thoroughness. Lord, she was so beautiful. The short white pleated skirt was fashioned of the softest, finest silk and shimmered in the moonlight. The white cashmere turtleneck sweater clung to the high curves of her breasts with a loving verity that revealed there was only Dany beneath its softness. Instead of her usual topknot, her auburn hair was loose and tumbling about her shoulders in a fiery cloak. He drew a deep breath. "I think you know you do. When you strut, you really strut, lady."

"There's no use making a halfway effort," she said lightly. "Anything I do I like to do intensely."

"Sometimes it's best to opt for moderation," he said warily. "I said the time of courtship, not mating, Dany."

"Did you?" she asked softly, her lashes suddenly veiling her eyes. "But surely there's nothing wrong in indulging me with another courtship ritual." She offered a quaint little curtsy. "Will you dance with me, Anthony?"

He chuckled. "We haven't skated pairs together in over six years. There's an excellent chance we'll end up in a heap on our respective rumps."

"Trust me." She held out her two hands invitingly. "And I'll trust you."

He became still. There had been an odd gravity in her voice that hinted at a depth of meaning other than the obvious. "Will you?" His hands reached out slowly to envelop her own. "Then how could I do less?" Stiffening his arms, he whirled her in a tight circle so that her hair flew out behind her in a bright satin banner. "It's an offer I can't refuse."

It took years and constant practice for a pairs team to acquire that magical merging of style and technique that was so sought after. Anthony should have been right about disaster following their own attempt after all these years. But somehow it didn't. It was smooth and beautiful and strangely, breathtakingly intimate. There were no spectacular overhead lifts, no death spirals. There was just Anthony holding her, lifting her in his arms, shifting her, whirling with her in a unity that filled her with a clear, radiant rapture. Silver moonlight on glittering silver blades, white pleats flowing silkily over black denim-covered thighs, haunting melody weaving shadow and brightness into one. Enchantment.

Dany wasn't sure at what point heart-lifting ecstasy became desire. It might have been during the pair sit-spin, when her thigh threaded between his, touched and burned. Or when he picked her up in his arms and cradled her with such tenderness that her throat ached with unshed tears. She was conscious only that desire was suddenly present, and she could feel in the abrupt tension of his arms that it was there for Anthony too.

She could see the jerky cadence of his pulse in his temple, and she knew that her own was just as uneven. The heat of his lean, supple body brushed against her with every movement, sensitizing her to a point where every touch was almost painful. His hand tightened spasmodically on her thigh, and he abruptly halted, pressing her close, his legs spreading to hold her within the cradle of his hips.

His chest was moving rapidly with the labor of his breathing as he held her quite still. "I think this particular courtship ritual had better stop," he said huskily.

"So do I." She turned her head so her lips were pressed against the pulse at the side of his warm throat. "I think we should move on to the mating." Not waiting for him to reply and ignoring the sudden stiffening of his body, she quickly covered his lips with hers in a lingering sweetness that escalated into explosive passion as she parted his lips with a tongue that ventured and then possessed.

He froze into immobility, and then she heard a low groan deep in his throat. Her tongue was met with his own in a kiss that probed and touched with a hot urgency. It was a long, breathless time before he jerked his head back, drawing in great gasps of air. "Calgary!"

She pressed closer, fitting her curves against his hard planes. "I'll *have* Calgary," she said fiercely. "And I'll have you too. I'll have it all."

"I told you—"

"You told me a lot of things." Her lips were moving over the warm skin of his throat. "I've stopped listening. They don't apply anymore."

"They don't?" He barely knew what he was saying. He could feel the curving softness of her unconfined breasts against him, and it was an agonizing temptation to slip his hand beneath the cashmere sweater and touch her, make her come alive for him.

"Nope." She nipped provocatively at the flesh just beneath his chin. "That was when you were controlling our relationship. Now it's strictly a joint project."

"Dany, I won't—"

"Yes, you will." She suddenly broke away from him with an impish laugh, backing a yard or so away. Her dark eyes were dancing. "I'm a very determined woman." Her hands were on her hips, toying with the edge of her sweater. "You've always given me whatever I wanted before. I don't see any reason why you should stop now." With one lightning movement she pulled the sweater over her head. Her breasts suddenly glimmered pale and full in the moonlight, their pink centers darkened and taut. "I remember how your hands felt on me, Anthony," she said softly. "Do you remember that? I want them on me again."

He remembered all right, and that memory was causing a painful tightness in his groin. "You'll get cold," he said gruffly.

"I don't think so." She smiled at him with loving sweetness. "I don't think you're about to let me get cold." She shook her long auburn hair so that it fell in a shimmering cascade over her shoulders and down her back. The sweater was still in her hand. "Here." She tossed him the garment. Then she was suddenly skating away from him toward the bench in the shadows at the end of the rink. "You can put it back on me when you catch me." She laughed again. "If you still want to!"

He stood there for a moment in the center of the rink, his hand clenching the softness of the cashmere. Now what the hell was he to do? This was a Dany he'd never known before, and he didn't know quite how to cope. It didn't help that he had to fight himself as well as her. Well, he couldn't let her wander around in the coolness of the rink half-dressed. He struck out with determined strokes toward the bench.

When he reached it, she was no longer there. Her white skates lay carelessly on the bench together with her boots and skate bag. How the hell had she gotten out of them so quickly? Now she was running around in only stocking feet, and the wooden floor was almost as cold as the ice. He sat down on the bench, quickly took off his own skates, and left them with hers, pushing his feet into loafers.

"Dany," he called in exasperation, his voice reverberating around the high ceiling of the building as he strode through the tiers of spectator seats. "Dany, dammit, answer me!"

There was a shimmering scrap of pleated material draped over a seat arm, and his hand reached out slowly to pick it up. Her skirt. He felt a swift jab of desire so intense, it was almost pure pain. "Dany!"

The sheer skater's tights were tossed carelessly on the railing leading to the lounge. He ignored them and moved toward the door with the numb heaviness of a sleepwalker.

He knew what he would see when he opened that door but still felt as if someone had kicked him in the stomach. She'd taken the wide cushions from the blue flowered couch and deposited them on the floor. She was sitting back on her heels at one end of the makeshift bed, her hands folded meekly in her lap, and her dark eyes glowing with tenderness in the lamplight. She was totally nude.

Dany felt the heat of his intense gaze as it ran over her body, and it brought a flush of arousal that swelled her breasts and caused her breath to catch in her throat. "I've heard that the chase always makes things more intriguing for a man," she said faintly. She mustn't feel shy, she told herself fiercely. How could she manage to seduce Anthony if she developed a case of nerves? "I thought

I'd give it a shot." She lifted her chin. "Are you intrigued, Anthony?"

"No, I'm not intrigued." He closed the door and leaned against it, his expression so intently sensual, it evoked a tingle in her every vein. "I'm angry and aroused." He paused. "And defeated." He dropped her sweater and skirt, and his fingers began to unfasten the belt at his waist. "You can put your own damn clothes on." He straightened and pulled his sweater over his head and tossed it aside. "Afterward."

Her eyes were suddenly enormous in her face as she watched him strip with his usual graceful economy of movement. "You're not really angry, are you?"

"What did you expect?" he asked as he moved across the room toward her. "I don't like to be forced into doing something against my better judgment."

"Am I forcing you?" she said falteringly as he knelt facing her. "I hoped I was seducing you."

"That too." A strand of fiery hair was curling over one naked breast as if it loved it. He wanted to push it aside and put his tongue there instead.

He was half afraid to touch her. He was holding on to his control with both hands. Desire was gnawing at him, and he was afraid he would turn into a wild animal. He didn't want to rape her, dammit. "I'm not sure I can be gentle with you," he said haltingly. "I've never wanted anyone this much before."

She relaxed. "Who said I wanted you to be gentle?" she asked lightly. "You've taught me to take care of myself, remember?"

His face suddenly softened. "This situation is a little different." His dark head bent and his lips brushed away the lock of hair from her nipple, stroking it lightly with his warm tongue. "This time we take care of each other." He suddenly pushed her back on the cushions, looking down at her with eyes that were smoky with desire. "Part your legs, love, I want to touch you."

Her limbs felt heavy and languid as she did what he asked. His face was taut and drawn with need and his eyes a deeper green than she'd ever seen them. He moved over her, his leg slipping between her own and nudging her open a little wider. His arms were resting on each side of her as his head came slowly down until his lips were hovering over her own. "Kiss me," he urged softly, rubbing his lower body against her with a slow undulation. "And I'll kiss you. Do you like that, Dany?"

"Oh, yes!" Her little gasp was lost against his lips as her arms went around his neck and pulled his head down so that she could give him her tongue as well as her mouth. He caught it between his lips, sucking and nipping erotically as his hips moved with a slowly rotating movement in that other embrace—one that was causing her to arch upward to tempt him to take more, to give more of himself.

She threw her head back to free her mouth so she could speak. "Anthony, I'm burning. . . ." His lips moved to take her again, and she felt his hands move between their bodies, petting and soothing that inferno, but it only served to stoke the flames. His fingers were playing, exploring, and she felt a deep clenching inside her. Then they invaded with a suddenness that made her cry out.

He raised his head swiftly. "Did I hurt you?" What he saw in her face reassured him. Surprise, languor, and a heavy sensuality, but no pain. His eyes narrowed on her face as he began to stroke, rotate, plunge. It was almost too much for him to bear to see the expressions of desire and heated need chase across her face as his fingers moved within her. Her gasps and little half moans were just as arousing. It filled him with a savage satisfaction that he could bring her to this peak of pleasure, but he knew he couldn't hold out much longer without taking his own fulfillment.

"You're ready for me," he said, his chest moving heavily with his labored breathing. He moved over her, and his manhood nudged against the center of her being. "And heaven knows, I'm ready for you, Dany." He tried to be slow and easy but she was so warm and tight, so very much *his* that suddenly he couldn't stand it.

He plunged forward with a force and fire that took her breath away. He was sheathed entirely within her, filling her, and there was an expression of such sensual contentment on the face above her that it made her own pleasure all the more intense. A lock of satin dark hair hung rakishly over his forehead and his eyes were shut as he flexed slowly and deeply.

She gave a half gasp and his eyes opened to look down at her with a lazy sensuousness. "I feel as if I've come home." There was a rare glint of mischief in his eyes. "You won't mind if I just stay here awhile and rest, will you, sweetheart?" He suddenly shifted so her thighs were over his and his hands were on her hips, pulling himself even deeper. "Remember, I said I wanted to learn you."

"Now?" she asked, her eyes widening. "Anthony, I don't think—" She broke off with a little gasp as she felt his hands on her, petting, moving, molding her around himself with a playfulness that was both loving and slightly savage. It was certainly, entirely mind-blowing, and she found herself panting and shivering with each teasing touch. She felt her hips suddenly rising and moving and she saw the teasing expression leave his face as he inhaled sharply.

He shifted and suddenly he was over her again. "I'll learn the rest later," he growled as he cupped her buttocks in his palms and tilted her up to him.

"There's going to be all the time in the world for both of us." He drew out and suddenly plunged forcefully forward, touching the center of her with explosive passion and beginning a rhythm that carried her into another universe.

The rhythm was like nothing she ever could have imagined. It was gone in an instant, it went on forever. It filled her body, it filled her heart. Burning sunlight on ice crystals, warming and then melting them so that both were one blazing spiral of urgency. Then the crystals reformed into a separate sharpness that was as breathlessly exquisite in sensation as the merging that had gone on before. Radiant prisms of brilliance intensified in color and beauty until they shattered into a million splinters of rapture.

The expression on Anthony's face above her was strained and taut and his chest was laboring with the harshness of his breathing as he rolled over, bringing her with him in that same possessive unity. "You're all right? I didn't hurt you?" His eyes were dark with concern as he looked at her.

"No." Her heart was pounding so fast she could hardly speak. "I'm fine. Are you okay?"

Amusement followed the relief on his face. "Never better," he assured her solemnly. "You were very gentle with me." His lips brushed her forehead with a tenderness that caused a lump to form in her throat. "But I wasn't the virgin here. You're an athlete, so I didn't think there'd be any pain, but I couldn't be sure. It worried the hell out of me."

"No pain." She nestled contentedly closer. "Only pleasure. I loved every minute of it. It was utterly fantastic." She nipped his shoulder playfully. "I could murder you for not making love to me at the apartment. We wasted three entire days."

He stiffened. "I thought it was wiser to wait." He pushed her away and sat up. "I still do." He rose from the bed of cushions with his customary litheness and stood looking down at her, all vulnerability and tenderness hidden behind his usual impassive mask. "I think we have a few things to discuss."

"Now?" she asked blankly as she watched him

retrieve his black sweater from the floor, then return to kneel beside her.

"Now," he said firmly. He sat her upright and pulled the sweater over her head, pushing her arms into the sleeves as if she were a little girl being dressed for school. "That little seduction scene you just pulled off makes me feel a good bit uneasy." He tugged the sweater down to her thighs and began rolling the overlong sleeves up to her elbow. He glanced up, his eyes more cool silver than green. "It makes me feel manipulated."

She nodded. "That's because you're not used to anyone else pulling the strings," she said cheerfully as she pushed the hair away from her face. "You're used to doing all the manipulating yourself." She crossed her legs tailor-fashion and grinned up at him mischievously. "How do you like it, Machiavelli?"

His lips tightened grimly. "I don't. It shouldn't have happened. Not yet."

"Bull," she said succinctly. "We're two consenting adults." Her eyes danced merrily. "At least you were very consenting a few moments ago. There's

173

no reason we shouldn't make love if we want to."
Her face softened. "And I wanted to."

"But *why* did you want to?" His eyes narrowed
on her face. "Lust, curiosity, a whim?" His face
darkened in a frown. "Or was it gratitude? Did
you suddenly decide to pay me for Briarcliff after
all? I told you—"

Her fingers swiftly covered his lips. "For good-
ness' sake, you certainly have a hangup about
that," she said crossly. "Look, I'm sorry I'm grateful to you. You've done so much for me, I'd be a
callous monster if I weren't. However, I certainly
didn't offer you my untouched body on any sacri-
ficial altar." She took her hand from his mouth.
"This untouched body wanted to be touched by
you, so I went about getting what it wanted in the
most logical way I could think of."

"Seduction."

"Exactly," she said with a satisfied smile. "And
you needn't think I'm paying you for Briarcliff,
because I'm going to deed it back to you as soon as
possible."

"No!" His frown deepened stormily. "That's

completely stupid. I don't care anything about the blasted place, and you do. It's yours, dammit."

"It will be someday," she said serenely. "After I win the gold and accept a contract with an ice show, I should have enough money to buy it from you. Until then it's yours, Anthony."

"I won't take it back," he growled, and for a moment he reminded her of a sulky little boy.

"You'll have to," she said lightly. "I'm a very independent lady. I only accept candy and flowers from my gentlemen friends." She fluttered her long lashes coyly. "Unlike another of Beau's southern literary ladies, 'Ah will not be dependent on the kindness of strangers.' "

"Strangers?" His lips curved sardonically. "After fourteen years, not to mention the intimacy we've known tonight, I'm scarcely a stranger, Dany."

"But you are," she said quietly. A beloved stranger, a stranger whose body excited her, whose mind challenged her, whose very presence drew her like a magnet, Dany told herself. "We've always been strangers, Anthony, because you wouldn't let me be anything else. Because I was too intimidated by you even to try to be anything else." She paused. "Past tense, you'll notice. I'm not afraid of you now. That's why I wanted you to make love to me tonight. I want to *know* you, Anthony."

"In the carnal sense?"

"In every sense." Her voice was grave. "You've dominated my life so long in so many ways. I feel so many things for you. I want to be able to sort them out, and I can't do that now. I *need* to do that."

"So you intend to become my mistress as some kind of psychological therapy?" She could almost feel the veil that surrounded his emotions harden and solidify. "I can't say that's exactly what I had in mind."

"I didn't think you did." Her eyes were clear and direct as they met his. "I think you wanted to retain your dominant position in our relationship because that would be the only way you'd also be able to maintain that barricade you put up between yourself and the rest of the world." She smiled a little sadly. "Oh, yes, you intended to encourage my independence, keep me content sexually, give me a small portion of yourself. Perhaps I would even have been happy for a little while. Until I realized what I was missing. Wasn't that the plan?"

"There wasn't any plan," he said absently, sitting back on his heels. He seemed supremely oblivious to his own strong, graceful nudity. "Though I might have had subconscious leanings in that direction." A tiny smile tugged at his lips. "And I'll promise you I'll keep you much more than content sexually. In case you didn't notice, we're pretty terrific together."

"I noticed," she said softly. Heavens, he was beautiful, Dany thought. The strong line of his thighs was pure singing grace, and the muscles of his chest and shoulders, while powerful, had a sleek suppleness that was a warm, tactile invitation. Suddenly she wanted to be back in his arms with an urgency that shocked her slightly. So soon? She drew a deep, steadying breath. "But it's not enough. I'm going to ask more from you than that." Her lips tightened determinedly. "No, I'm going to demand it."

"Demand." He repeated the word as if it left a sour taste on his tongue. "I don't believe I like the nuances in that word. You'd get a great deal further with me by asking. I don't particularly appreciate that touch of aggressiveness in you, Dany."

"Don't you? Jack likes it very much," she said with deliberate provocation. "He appreciates a good many of the more liberated facets of my personality." She watched the swift frown that darkened Anthony's face with almost objective curiosity. "But then, we're very open with each other. That has a way of breeding"—she paused before adding—"intimacy."

"I know what you're doing, you know," he said curtly, his eyes flashing. "Jealousy is the oldest ploy in history, and you're not being overly subtle."

"I'm not trying to be. I'm just pointing out that if you're not willing to give me what I want, there are other men who will." She looked away so that he wouldn't see the tenderness mixed with pain in her eyes. She didn't want any other man. Only Anthony—for the rest of her life. Only Anthony. "Men who are willing to give more of themselves than a token."

"The bottom line, Dany?" The crispness of his

tone was belied by the smoldering flicker in his eyes. "You're leading up to something. I want the bottom line."

"The bottom line is that I'm going to own you body and soul," she said simply. "And if you'll let me do that, I'll let you own me in the same way." Her gaze returned to regard him steadily. "And if you don't, we're going to have to say good-bye. I wouldn't be able to bear it any other way."

"You make it sound so damn easy," he said harshly. "I told you I'm not a generous man where my feelings are concerned." His face was shadowed with strain. "I *can't* give you what you want. I don't know if I'll ever be able to. There's something inside me that won't let go. Don't you think I'd like to be as open and uncomplicated as that son of a bitch Kowalt?"

Oh, dear heaven, how she loved him. She felt a rush of maternal tenderness so intense, it was almost painful. She wanted to take him in her arms and soothe away the pain she felt in him, to tell him it was all right, that she'd accept whatever he could give her. No. She mustn't do that. She'd be cheating them both of their chance to have it all if she gave in now.

"Then I'll teach you," she said, keeping her voice steady with an effort. "You've taught me any number of things over the years." She smiled shakily. "After all, turnabout is only fair play. It'll work."

"And if it doesn't?" His voice was rough. "If you think I'm going to let you go, you're sadly mistaken."

"Let me try. At least let me try," she whispered. "Just promise that you won't get angry and close up when I probe, when I won't let you shut me out."

He was silent for a long moment, and she could feel the tension in him reaching out to her. "You're a determined little thing, aren't you?" he asked jerkily. "Okay, I'll do my best." Then, as she smiled delightedly, he added, "But you're not getting everything your own way. I'm taking out a little insurance just in case you can't turn me into Mr. Warm and Wonderful."

"Insurance?"

He nodded. "Propinquity, intimacy, and sex

constitute an umbrella policy that's pretty darn unbeatable. You just might find after two weeks of constant inundation that you may not want to be quite so adamant in your demands."

"Two weeks?" Her brow knotted in puzzlement. "I still don't understand."

"We're going away together for the next two weeks," he said coolly. "I have a lodge in the White Mountains I use occasionally. It's very small and completely isolated. There's not even a telephone. There's a pond on the property that always stays frozen this time of year, and we can use it to keep you in shape and correct those rough places in your routine." He smiled slightly. "I can assure you, you won't overtrain up there. You'll be spending too much time in bed."

"Do you think that's wise?" Dany asked hesitantly. "I'll have to leave immediately for Calgary after those two weeks. Will I be ready?"

"It's a little late to think of that now. I told you where my priorities would lie if I ever made love to you." His eyes were moving over her, lingering on her pert breasts beneath the black wool of the sweater. "You first, the gold second. You made the choice."

"You don't mean that," she said quietly. "You want that gold as much as I do. You wouldn't let me lose it this late in the game."

"Wouldn't I?" His lips twisted. "How would you know what a 'stranger' would do?" Then he shrugged wearily. "I hope to heaven I wouldn't. I think I'm right about the overtraining. If I am, this is the best move you could make." His eyes met hers. "On the other hand, I could be rationalizing to give myself an excuse to put you where I've wanted you for the last six years. You'd better consider that."

She shook her head. "I won't consider it," she said firmly. "Not for a minute. I trust you, Anthony."

"That's more than I do myself," he said dryly. "I hope you won't regret it."

"I won't," she said with a serene smile. "When do we leave?"

"Tomorrow morning," he said absently. "Late morning. We aren't going to get much sleep tonight." He reached for the bottom of the sweater that was hugging her thighs. "I can see these pretty nipples standing up and pushing against this. The wool is irritating them, isn't it?"

"I didn't noti—" She broke off as the sweater was pulled swiftly over her head and tossed aside.

Then he was leaning forward, his dark head bent, his warm tongue gently moving over the tips of her breasts. "Does this make them feel better, Dany?" he asked thickly, nipping and suckling at the sensitive tips. His hand was between her legs, petting her with a deliciously sensual skill. "Is that what you want?"

She jerked as he touched her with sudden erotic force that sent her rocketing into a volcano of heat. "Yes, that's what I want."

He was bearing her back on the cushions, his expression intent and heavy. "Just relax. I want to make it last a long time this time. I want to give you so much pleasure that you'll go crazy with it." His hand shaped and molded one firm breast with lazy skill. "I'm going to find out what you like and what you don't." His lips lowered and he blew on the moist, rosy tip. "Everything."

She felt a fire shoot from his manipulating

hand to the center of her womanhood and the tingle of urgency begin. "Insurance?" she gasped faintly.

"Oh, yes," he agreed as his hand moved over to the other breast and clasped it with the same exciting possession. "Insurance, Dany. Insurance of the very best kind."

Chapter 6

The snowflakes were beginning to fall at a much faster pace now, no longer star-shaped flutters that glittered here and there on the ice. It was time for Dany to come in, dammit.

Anthony jammed his hands in the pockets of his sheepskin jacket and called again from the snow-covered bank. "Dany, that's enough. We've got to get back to the lodge." He knew how Dany always got wrapped up once she hit the ice. Look at her, he mused—whirling and leaping as if the surface were glass-smooth instead of becoming increasingly rough with every passing minute. He'd just opened his lips to call again when she turned and waved and the words died unspoken.

God, she was lovely; all fire and grace and vitality. The navy blue of the skating skirt and matching ski sweater made her auburn hair, caught back in a ponytail, come alive with sparkling highlights as she whirled. Her face was glowing with exuberance and a touch of that dreamy exultation he'd seen on it so long ago. He felt something melt deep inside him, and he knew an aching tenderness. Dany was gathering stars again. Perhaps just a little longer wouldn't hurt. A triple, a double axel, a layback spin, and then she was suddenly skating toward him. The snowflakes were drifting around her like a curtain of stars, but she wasn't reaching out for them now. Her dark eyes were alight with mischief as she skated to a stop before him with a little flourish.

"Hi, I know who you are. You're Anthony Malik and you won a gold medal. I'm going to win one someday too." She paused. "And then everybody's going to love me." Her face was almost luminous. "Isn't that the way it went, Anthony? And then you said . . . ?"

He knew what she wanted him to say. Oh, God, he *did* love her. It was as if that little girl she had been and the desirable temptress she was now had merged into one. He loved her in so many ways that sometimes he felt as if it were consuming him. Why was it so hard to tell her?

"We'd better get back to the lodge," he said gruffly. "The radio predicted heavy snow for this afternoon and evening. You're not going to get any decent practice for the rest of the day." He reached out, lifted her onto the bank, and knelt to quickly unlace her skates. "The temperature is falling too. You should have worn your jumpsuit."

"I like to wear skirts," she said absently, looking down at his dark head bent over the skates. There had been something so open and vulnerable in his eyes as she'd skated toward him that it had caused her heart to leap with hope. Now he was closing up again. It had happened a dozen times in the week they'd been at the lodge, and she supposed she should be used to it. Just when she could see the barrier between them melting, he would erect another defense. It was only because she'd been so happy that the rejection meant so much today. Her voice was sharp as much from pain as exasperation. "I'm not cold. You're the one who's cold."

He took her skates and placed them carefully in the skate bag, his head still bent as he slipped her boots on her feet. "I'm fine. This jacket's very warm," he said, deliberately misunderstanding her. His hand had moved from her ankle with slow provocation up her leg to rub her inner thigh with a teasing sensuality. His hand was warm on her cold flesh, and it sent a shock of heat through her. She went still and felt her breath catch in her throat. His voice was silkily seductive. "Don't worry, you'll be warm, too, when I get you back to the lodge." He bent forward to brush his lips to the flesh he'd just sensitized. "But then, you're always warm"—his teeth nipped gently—"and sweet and . . ."

No, she wouldn't let him do this to her. It always ended this way when they came too close to a confrontation. He used sex with a blinding skill that made her forget everything but the pleasure he gave her. But not today. Her hand went to his head and pulled it back, the thick crispness of his hair on her palm giving her another little tactile jolt. "Yes, I'm warm," she said deliberately. "I'm warm because you mean so much to me. I can't help myself." Her eyes were grave as they looked into his. "Do you want me to say it first? Will that help you? I love you." She could see his eyes flicker with an emotion that could have been either joy or surprise. Perhaps a little of both, Dany thought. "But it's lonely standing out here on a limb by myself. I need company." Her voice had the slightest quaver in it. "I need you to say you love me too."

She could see the struggle that brought the strain back to his face. He glanced away as he asked evasively, "What's not to love?" He got to his feet and picked up her skate bag. "You're gorgeous, intelligent, and more responsive than any lady I've ever slept with. I'd be an idiot not to love you."

"Damn you!" Her voice was shaking with the force of her feelings. She felt as if he'd slapped her. Her eyes were bright with unshed tears. "I'm tired of your blasted evasions and your charming little sexual insurance policies. Just once, couldn't you have given me *something*? Damn you!" Then she was running up the hill, her booted feet slipping on the new snow. The snow felt wet on her face—or was it tears? No, she wouldn't cry. She wouldn't let him hurt her. He didn't mean to, she knew that. She should be more patient. She always meant to be, but sweet heaven, how long could she batter against that wall of reserve without breaking apart herself?

Then she was inside the small redwood chalet, almost running down the hall to the sauna area. She was freezing, shaking more from the chill of frustrated emotions than the temperature. Anthony hadn't followed, and it didn't really surprise her. He knew that, as upset as she was, she'd never allow him to avoid another confrontation. He'd probably wait for her to calm down, then step in and attempt to soothe her with humor, and gentleness, and that universal panacea he was so damn good at.

And she'd probably let him! Once the first agony had worn away, she'd be willing to try again. She'd discovered in the past week that the little Anthony gave her was better than no Anthony at all. Any threat to the effect of leaving him now would be pure bluff. She could only hope he wouldn't realize that. It was the only weapon she had.

She stood in the combination bathing–sauna area now, shedding her clothes swiftly and leaving them where they fell on the cream-and-jade ceramic tile floor. She'd pick them up later. She had a sudden poignant memory of Anthony's meticulousness as opposed to her own haphazardness. He'd quietly pick up her clothes and hang them up with simple matter-of-factness. She'd thought her carelessness would grate on his nerves, but he'd never shown by word or expression that that might be the case. He'd accepted every facet of her personality without question or criticism. Why couldn't she do the same? It would be a hell of a lot less painful.

Dany decided against going into the pine-enclosed sauna cubicle and chose the hot tub instead. It would warm her more quickly, and she needed that. Lord, she needed that. She felt frozen to the marrow. The water was blessedly hot as she settled onto the bench and leaned her head back against the side of the tub. Her eyes closed as she let the swirling waters ease and comfort her as the tension loosened and flowed away with the heat and the steam. She wished the pain could flow away as easily. Perhaps it would in time. Maybe it wouldn't matter as much next month or next year.

"Dany."

Anthony was suddenly beside her in the tub. She could feel the water ebb as he settled himself beside her. She hadn't heard him, but that wasn't surprising. Anthony always moved with such swift, silent grace.

She tensed, not opening her eyes. "Go away," she said huskily. "I don't want to see you. Not now."

"Then keep your eyes shut." His voice was ragged. "Because I'm not going to go away." His arms wrapped around her, cradling her with infinite gentleness. "In fact, I'd prefer you didn't open them; it will make it easier for me." His clasp tightened. "Just stop crying, okay?"

"I'm not crying," she denied. "It's just perspiration."

"Is it?" His tongue licked delicately at her cheek in a tenderly intimate gesture before his hand pulled her head into the hollow of his shoulder. "I don't think so."

"I wish you'd just go away." His hand was stroking her back and shoulders with soothing tenderness, and she could feel herself begin to melt against him. "I don't want to have sex with you."

"We never have sex." His voice was muffled as he pressed his lips to her forehead. "We make love. Even if I had trouble saying the words, I thought you knew that. And I don't want to do that either. Not right now."

She became still. "You don't?"

"For God's sake, what kind of bastard do you think I am?" There was a thread of pain in his voice. "You're hurting, don't you think I know that? I want to comfort you. I don't *take* a hundred percent of the time." He laughed mirthlessly. "Only ninety-five percent."

"No," she protested. She tried to raise her head, but he stopped her with a firm pressure that kept it cradled on his shoulder. "I know you can't help it."

"Then I'd better try, hadn't I? Because I sure as hell can't stand to see that look on your face again. It nearly tore me apart." His voice sank to a halting whisper. "I—I love you, Dany."

This time he didn't stop her when she raised her head, her lids flying open to stare at him with startled eyes. His face was a little pale, the skin stretched taut over the broad planes of his cheekbones, but his eyes were direct and steady as they met hers.

"You're sure?" she whispered.

There was a flicker of impatience in his face. "If I wasn't, do you think I would have said it?" he growled. "It's not exactly a declaration I make every day. Do you want me to repeat it?"

She felt such a surge of joy, it left her lightheaded. Oh, Lord, the first rip in the veil. She was sure that if she stood up, she'd float away on a fleecy cloud of sheer euphoria. "I'm not about to press my luck," she said lightly. Her eyes were glowing with a radiance that made his breath catch in his throat. "You almost didn't make it that time. I'll be satisfied if you manage to drop it casually into the conversation every year or so."

He tilted her head up to him, his palms cradling her cheeks with velvet gentleness. "I think I'll be able to do better than that." He kissed her with a sweetness that was neither victory nor defeat, but a magical compromise of the spirit. "I imagine it will be easier with practice." He brushed a butterfly kiss on each eyelid. "I love you. See? That wasn't very rusty at all."

"Don't push it, you're doing fine." She cuddled happily against him, her lips pressing extravagant little kisses over his throat and shoulders. "It's more than enough for right now."

"I'm glad you're so pleased, but I'd appreciate it if you'd stop expressing yourself quite so enthusiastically," he said with a chuckle. "I'm trying to demonstrate how loving, not lustful, I can be." As her head nestled contentedly back on his shoulder his hand stroked her hair back from her temple. "I thought when you were tired of this, we'd get dressed and sit in front of the fire and talk or play cards or whatever else you want to do. Does that sound all right?"

It sounded wonderful, she thought happily—as wonderful as being held with exquisite care, as if she were very precious; as wonderful as being told by Anthony Malik that she was loved. She didn't fool herself that the war was by any means won, but it was a major victory all the same. "Okay," she said dreamily, breathing in the clean scent of musk and soap that always surrounded him. "Anthony?" Her voice was hesitant. "What made you tell me? Why now?"

There was a short silence. "I couldn't bear it," he said finally. "Anything was better than seeing that expression on your face. You looked as if I'd stolen one of your stars."

"Stars?"

His hand was once more stroking her temple with mesmerizing gentleness. "Never mind." His lips feathered kisses on her forehead. "It doesn't matter."

"I'm getting better, aren't I?" Dany tossed her jacket on the bench by the front door and whirled in a circle, hugging herself ecstaticallly. "I could *feel* it today. I was part of everything—the ice, the wind, the music. Everything."

Anthony closed the door behind him and shrugged out of his jacket. "You were better today than yesterday," he said cautiously. "You could have had more height on that split. . . ."

"Anthony, dammit, I was good," she said with loving impatience. "Admit it!" She wrinkled her nose at him. "And I'll admit that you were right about the overtraining. Though it goes against my grain to add to your arrogant ego."

He picked up her jacket and opened the hall closet. His back was to her as he carefully hung up both their coats and put her skate bag in the closet. His voice was slightly muffled. "All right, I'll admit it. You were fantastic. Satisfied?"

"No." Her hand was on his arm, swiveling him around to confront her. "I want to see your face when you say it." Her dark eyes were dancing. "Now, wasn't I absolutely wonderful today?"

His expression softened as he gazed down at her eager face. "You were beautiful," he said simply. "If you do that well at Calgary, you'll wrap up the gold and take it home." His fingers gently traced the curve of her cheekbone. "You were everything I knew you could be. If I had a thousand gold medals, I would have given them all to you today." He inclined his head in a mocking little bow. "Is that better, sweetheart?"

"Yes, that's better," she said huskily. She cleared her throat, and her arms slipped around him to give him a hug that took his breath away. "You did that very well. You're learning all the time." Before his arms could close around her, she was whirling away again. "In fact, I think that effort deserves a reward. I'll make you a cup of hot chocolate before we start dinner." She grinned at him teasingly. "I hope you appreciate the sacrifice. After all, I'm the one who slaved away on the ice all afternoon while you lolled on the bank like some royal potentate and watched."

"We all have our roles to play," he drawled as he turned and straightened her jacket on the hanger. "I find my sultan to your slave girl a very satisfying match."

"I wish you wouldn't pick up after me," Dany said with a grimace as he closed the closet door and turned around to face her. "It always makes me feel like such a complete slob." She hurried on defensively, "I would have picked up everything and hung it up later, you know."

"Sorry. I didn't realize it bothered you." His arm wrapped around her waist as he propelled her down the hall toward the country kitchen in the rear of the lodge. "I'll try to remember, though I don't promise anything. Neatness is an ingrained habit with me. My first twelve years were spent in a two-room tenement apartment. If I didn't keep things picked up, it was even more of a disaster area than it usually was." His lips tightened. "And God knows, that was bad enough."

It was the first time she'd ever heard Anthony speak about his childhood. He'd never made any secret of the fact he'd grown up in poverty, but he kept the details of his upbringing as strictly confidential as the rest of his past.

"That must have been very difficult for you." Her eyes were thoughtful. "I can see how my carelessness must have annoyed you."

"It never annoyed me," he said, surprised. "Growing up as you did, your habits are as natural to you as mine are to me. We all develop as our environment dictates."

"You didn't," she said softly. "Growing up in a

tenement, you shouldn't have gotten nearly as far as you did. How do you explain that?"

"Let's just say I had a few other inducements besides poverty to break free of my environment," he said evasively. He settled down into the corner breakfast booth and lazily stretched out his legs before him. "Now what were you saying about that hot chocolate, slave?"

The subject was closed. Nothing could be clearer, and Dany turned away to the cabinet with an exasperated toss of her head. She shouldn't be so impatient, she knew. In the past few days Anthony had been more open and giving to her than ever before. He'd talked of his work as head of Dynathe, regaled her with amusing anecdotes of his life as the star of the Ice Revue. He'd even spoken briefly and unemotionally of Samuel Dynathe, who'd seen him skate in a charity-sponsored competition when Anthony was twelve and had become his patron and later his employer. But there were some subjects he just wouldn't discuss, and one of them was his life before Dynathe appeared on the scene. It was perfectly maddening, because

Dany had an idea the key to Anthony's reserve lay in the details of that period.

She still knew only the facets of Anthony's personality and life he chose to share with her. If his manner was gradually becoming warmer and easier with her every day, it was something for which she was fervently grateful. But there were far too many sharp edges still. Foremost among them was his almost fanatic and incomprehensible insistence that need and gratitude had no place in their relationship, and his icy jealous rage whenever she mentioned Jack Kowalt. In moments like those she realized just how far they still had to go before they reached a total understanding.

She set a small saucepan on the stove and turned to the refrigerator to get the milk. "I'm sure the appearance of Samuel Dynathe on the scene must have made a difference," she said with deceptive casualness. "From what you told me, he wouldn't have wanted his protégé to damage his image. It must have been the male equivalent of the Cinderella story." She poured the milk into the saucepan and turned the burner on low. "What did your parents think of it all?"

"Drop it, Dany." His voice was so harsh and incisive, she cast a startled glance over her shoulder at him. His expression was even harder than his voice, his silver-green eyes bleak and cold. "I don't feel like putting up with your amateur psychologist probing at the moment."

"I just wanted—"

"I know what you wanted to do," he interrupted roughly. "How the hell could I help it? You're just like a bull terrier when you get your mind set on something. You want to save me from myself or some such rot." His smile was distinctly unpleasant. "Before you concern yourself with my hang-ups, I'd suggest you exorcise your own."

She carefully took the saucepan off the burner and turned slowly to face him. "What do you mean?"

"That never-ending search for love and approval. Everyone has to love Dany Alexander, don't they? Beau, Marta, Kowalt, me. We all have to make up for the affection and attention you never received from your parents. Even the gold isn't going to be a reward for achievement so much as a bribe to the whole damn world." He laughed harshly. "That's what you told me, remember? 'I'm going to win the gold someday and then everybody's going to love me.'"

She shivered as she folded her arms across her chest. Every word he spoke tore at her like tiny knives. Was he right? Was she demanding more than she should from everyone around her because of some desperate craving for attention? "Yes, I remember," she whispered, her face suddenly pale and haunted. "I guess I never realized that I was like that."

His expression suddenly changed and he was on his feet and across the room in a few rapid steps. "That's because it's not true." His arms enfolded her with a tenderness that was a balm to the rawness of the wound. His lips pressed against her temple and he began rocking her as if she were a hurt little girl. "That's because you're sweet and beautiful and naturally loving." His voice was muffled in her hair. "Which makes you a choice target for bastards like me. You don't have any armor to defend yourself with and every barb strikes home."

"But perhaps you were right." Her voice was troubled. "Maybe I am—"

"I wasn't right," he said roughly. "You made me angry and I struck back instinctively." He was suddenly lifting her and carrying her over to the booth. "And my instincts aren't always civilized. Occasionally I revert to the doctrine of the streets. Where I grew up, any punch—clean or dirty—was applauded if it brought the other guy down." He sat down on the edge of the bench and cradled her in his arms. "That one was definitely a low blow, Dany."

The rawness was gradually disappearing under his gentleness. "Well, it was certainly effective," she said shakily as she settled her cheek into her favorite place beneath his collarbone. "It sort of took my breath away."

"I know, I could see it." His voice beneath her ear was husky. "If it's any comfort, I think it hurt me more than it did you. I always seem to be putting my foot in my mouth."

"Impossible," she said lightly. "Not our silver-tongued tycoon, the diplomat of the boardroom."

"It's different with you." His hand moved to

the elastic of her ponytail, and her hair was suddenly tumbling to her shoulders. "I *care* about you."

"I thought I'd weaned you away from those euphemisms." Her lips pressed to the hollow in his throat. "Say it, dammit."

"I love you." His arms tightened around her with crushing force. "I *do* love you. Lord, I'm sorry, sweetheart."

"That was very satisfactory," she said shakily. "Just the right note of sincerity. See that you keep it up. As you may have noticed, I need that kind of treatment very frequently."

"I'm much better at demonstrations." His lips were pulling gently at her earlobe. "Let's go to bed."

She tilted her head back to meet his eyes in surprise. There had been nothing in the least sensual in his demeanor, only that lovely gentleness that shone so brightly in contrast to the sharpness that had gone before. "Now?"

"Now," he said softly. "I want to make love to you. I want to know I've erased those words from your mind. I want to give you so much pleasure, you'll forget I ever said them. I want to *give* to you, Dany." His voice held a desperate honesty. "I may not be able to give you the pretty phrases you need, but I can show you how I feel. Making love is one thing I know well."

"So I've observed." There was a twinkle in her eyes despite the tightness of her throat. "It's not necessary, you know. I wouldn't want to cause you any undue hardship."

He ignored her flippancy, his tone intense. "I don't think you really believed me before. It's not just sex. When I make love to you, it means something. Will you let me show you?"

"If it means that much to you," she said, a little throatily.

"It does mean that much." He rose to his feet with her in his arms and strode swiftly out of the kitchen toward the bedroom. "It means a hell of a lot."

When she thought about that afternoon later, it was with a strange, dreamlike ecstasy. The entire period was a contrast of sharp contours and soft hazy fragments that merged together into an unforgettable whole. The dimness of the bedroom that shadowed Anthony's face above her made the silver-green of his eyes glow flamelike. Dany felt the touch of soft, skillful lips on her thighs; his hands, sensitive to every nuance of response, traveled over her with a magical tenderness so moving, she felt the tears brim and then roll slowly down her cheeks. He knew how to please her now, and he took his time, arousing and then checking any number of times so that her passion would build to a summit of sensation so intense, it couldn't be stemmed. Then, when they were both breathless and shaking from a completion that was as wildly exciting as the anticipation she had felt before, he would begin again.

He murmured husky words in her ear.

"Do you like that, love?"

"Shall I touch you there a little longer?"

"I love it when you cry out like that. I want to make you do it again. Oh, yes, that sounds so sweet."

"Tell me if you like this. It's a little different, but . . . ah, I thought you would."

It went on and on, words of sweet desire that

held no vestige of his usual dominant aggressiveness. He'd said he wanted to pleasure her, and he went about it with an almost boyish eagerness. He seemed to delight in every cry or gasp of fulfillment that broke from her, refusing with gentle firmness to let her give him a similar pleasure.

Late afternoon had faded into twilight and then into early evening when Anthony finally settled her against his shoulder in an embrace that was lovingly affectionate. His fingers combed lazily through her hair with a hypnotic, soothing motion. "You see, I'm much better at demonstrations."

"I'm not about to argue that point," she said drowsily. "I may never ask you to open your mouth again." She suddenly chuckled. "Except for the use to which you so recently put it."

"I thought you'd qualify that," he said, amused. "You did appear to enjoy yourself exceedingly."

"Oh, yes." She sighed. "Definitely yes."

"Good." For a moment there was a thread of that former desperation in his tone. "That's what I wanted. Now, whatever happens, you'll know I can at least give you that."

She felt a stir of uneasiness. This moment was so beautiful, she didn't want any element of strife to shatter it. "Well, there was one little problem."

She felt him stiffen against her. "I did something you didn't like?"

"Are you kidding? You'd have to be mentally defective not to realize how much I loved everything you were doing to me." She paused. "It's just that I feel guilty as the devil you wouldn't let me give you the same pleasure."

He relaxed. "Some other time," he said lightly, "I'll keep the offer in mind." He hesitated. "There is one thing you could do for me." There was a trace of mischief in his voice that so rarely surfaced.

She answered warily. "Really? What's that?"

"If you think I've earned it, could I have my hot chocolate now?"

Chapter 7

"Are you sure you're feeling all right?" Dany asked anxiously as she set Anthony's cup of coffee on the table by the couch. "You scarcely touched your dinner."

"I'm fine," he said, a touch of impatience in his voice. "That's the third time you've asked me that this evening. What does it take to convince you, for heaven's sake? I just wasn't hungry."

She winced. She wasn't used to that razor sharpness in Anthony's tone any longer, and it hurt. "Sorry," she said in a subdued tone as she sat down beside him on the couch. "It's just that you've been so quiet all day and you didn't eat much for lunch either."

"That doesn't necessarily mean that I'm at death's door," he said caustically. "I do have a few things to think about, you know. One of which is how to get you to concentrate on those compulsory figures. The tracings on that second set were rotten. We have to return to Briarcliff tomorrow and you'll leave for Calgary the day after. Time's running out, and you're still acting as if you can breeze right through the Olympics as if it were a regional competition."

She bristled. "You're the one who told me I was overtraining. You can't have it both ways, Anthony."

"You're not going to have it any way at all if you mess up the compulsories so that you go into the freestyle with too much ground to make up," he said grimly. "Those judges are tough as hell, and nationalism definitely enters into the picture, despite what the committee will tell you."

"I know all that," she said, her lips trembling. "I also know I get impatient occasionally and screw up on the compulsories. I thought I was getting better about it, though. Were they that bad, Anthony?"

"They weren't good." He picked up his cup and took a sip of coffee. He made a face and set the cup back on the saucer. "That tastes terrible. What the devil did you put in it?"

There was no pleasing him tonight, she thought crossly. "Next time I'll let you make it yourself, since it appears you're the authority on everything around here."

"Do that," he said curtly. "If you can't do something right, it's better not to do it at all."

"So speaks the great perfectionist. Doesn't your halo ever get a little heavy, Anthony?"

"If you don't maintain—" He stopped suddenly and shook his head as if to clear it. "Good God, what the hell am I saying?" His hand combed through his hair distractedly. "You're right, I sound like some third-rate dictator."

"My thought exactly." She drew a deep, shaky breath. "And I didn't think the workout today was all that bad."

"What?" He glanced at her absently. "No, you

were fine," he said vaguely as he got to his feet. "I'm thirsty. I think I'll go to the kitchen and get a glass of water." He strode out of the room, leaving her to gaze after him with puzzled eyes.

She grew more puzzled and anxious as the evening wore on. There was no question now that there was something very wrong with Anthony, despite his protests to the contrary. His eyes were unnaturally bright and there was an unhealthy flush on his cheeks. He was obviously trying to control his mental processes, but his attempts at conversation often disintegrated into incoherence as he seemed to drift away. In a person as incisive as Anthony, that frightened Dany more than any of the other signs.

Since she couldn't get him to admit anything was wrong, she pleaded weariness and chose to make it an early night, hoping that she could get him to rest.

When she came out of the shower, he was already in bed, lying stiff and still on his side of the double bed. His eyes were feverishly brilliant in his flushed face, and his dark hair was tousled. She took off her flowered peach silk robe and slipped under the sheet. For the first time since they'd come to the lodge, he didn't reach out for her. She suddenly felt very cold and lonely. "Anthony?" she whispered. "Can I get you something? Maybe an aspirin or a hot drink?"

"Nothing." His voice was rigidly controlled. "I told you I was fine. Turn off the lamp."

"But there's something *wrong*." She felt so damn helpless. "Perhaps you've caught a cold."

"I haven't caught a cold," Anthony said with certainty. "And there's nothing you can do to help. Now, will you turn out that damn light or shall I?"

"I'll do it." She reached out and pressed the switch of the lamp on the bedside table. Oh, Lord, there *was* something wrong. Why wouldn't he admit it and let her help? Was he really ill? She felt a cold rush of panic touch her heart. There was a particularly virulent strain of flu going around that was often accompanied by pneumonia.

"Anthony, why don't—"

"There's nothing wrong with me," he interrupted with icy precision. "Good night, Dany."

"Good night," she murmured unhappily. She

closed her eyes but could feel the tears burning behind her lids. He mustn't be sick, she thought frantically. She'd die if anything happened to Anthony now. He was lying so still, his body unnaturally rigid, and even though she wasn't touching him, she was conscious of the heat emanating from him. Fever?

She lay there in miserable silence for what seemed hours, but she must have dozed off finally. The next thing she heard was Anthony's voice uttering soft curses in her ear and she lifted her head from his shoulder in sleepy bewilderment. Sometime during the night she must have rolled over and cuddled close to him, as was her custom. But there was something horribly different about him. "You're shaking," she said, sitting bolt upright in bed. Her eyes widening in alarm, she reached out and touched his shoulder. His flesh was so hot and dry that she inhaled sharply. "Anthony, you're burning up. You must have a chill."

"No, not a chill," he muttered. "I thought I could fight it off. Sometimes I can." Suddenly he was sitting up and swinging his legs off the bed. "Don't worry, I'll take care of it."

"Take care of what?" She switched on the light to see him putting on his clothes with a haste that was hampered by the clumsiness of his movements. Clumsy? Anthony was always incredibly graceful. It was almost obscene to see that awkwardness in him now. Her throat tightened in fear. "Please come back to bed. You're sick, Anthony. For heaven's sake, *listen* to me."

"I'll be all right," he mumbled as he pulled his sweater over his head. He staggered a little and then steadied. "I'll take care of it."

She was out of bed, yanking on her robe. "You're not all right. Let me help you. I think we'd better get a doctor."

"I don't need any help." He was at the closet, pulling out his sheepskin coat. "I never need any help."

"You do now." She was beside him and she tried to take the jacket from him. "You can't go out when you're burning up with fever. Go back to bed and I'll make you comfortable. Then I'll drive down to the nearest town and bring back a doctor."

"No, I'll go." He jerked the jacket from her and shrugged into it. "Go back to bed. I'll send Beau up tomorrow to get you."

"Go back to . . . ?" She couldn't believe it. He expected her calmly to go back to bed and go to sleep when she was practically frantic with worry! "Well both go, then." She turned to the closet and yanked a sweater and a pair of jeans off the hangers. "I'll be with you in just a minute."

But he was already out of the bedroom and lurching unsteadily down the hall toward the front door. "Anthony, dammit, wait for me!" She clutched the jeans and sweater in her arms and ran after him. "You can't drive yourself. That road down the mountain has hairpin curves. Even if you were well, it would be dangerous in the dark. Sick as you are, it would be suicide." She grabbed him by the shoulder as he opened the door and a frigid blast of air invaded the hall. "Just for once, why can't you give in and admit you need someone, that you need *me*?"

He shook off her hold and turned to look down at her, his eyes reflecting only a burning ferocity in the stark harshness of his face. "Because I don't

need you. I don't need *anyone,* and I never will."
He strode out of the lodge, leaving her to stare
after him in stunned agony.

Then she heard the soft roar of the Mercedes
and she was galvanized into action at the thought
of Anthony trying to negotiate those deadly
curves.

"No!" She ran out of the lodge toward the
garage at the side of the chalet, but he'd already
backed the Mercedes out and had started down
the driveway. She ran after him, slipping on the
ice and snow. "Anthony, stop!"

The car was picking up speed, and she finally
stopped when she realized pursuit was useless.
Her breath was coming in little painful gasps. She
wasn't even aware of the tears running down
her cheeks or the flimsiness of her robe that was
her only protection against the frigid cold. She
watched the taillights disappear around a curve.
"Anthony!"

She was still wearing the flowered robe when she
opened the door for Beau the next afternoon. The

tears, however, had long since dried, to be replaced by numb despair.

"He made it down the mountain, then." It was a statement, not a question. He'd said he'd send Beau to get her, and he'd kept his promise. If he'd catapulted off the mountain, it would have been the highway patrol knocking on the door. She'd been expecting that knock through all those nightmarish hours since Anthony left.

"He made it." Beau's eyes were warm with sympathy. "Though God knows how. I had trouble negotiating some of those turns myself on the way up here." He stepped into the hall and closed the door behind him. "He called me from the hospital and told me to get up here and take care of you."

"Hospital!" Panic roused her briefly from her apathy. "Anthony's in a hospital?"

"Only for a few days," Beau said soothingly. "He'll be out as soon as the fever goes down. It usually never gets this far. It wouldn't have this time if he'd brought his quinine with him." His hand reached out to touch her cheek with affection. "You should be flattered. He obviously wasn't thinking of anyone but you when he left Briarcliff. That's not like Anthony at all."

"Why should he have to take quinine with him?" she asked, brushing his hand away impatiently. "What's wrong with him, Beau?"

"Malaria," he said, surprised. "Didn't he tell you last night?"

"No, he didn't tell me," she said dully. "He didn't tell me anything. Malaria! How, for heaven's sake?"

"He got the bug several years ago in South America when we were touring with the Ice Revue." He frowned thoughtfully. "I think it was in Brasília." He shrugged. "Anyway, it was a pretty bad case. Malaria victims are subject to relapses because the bug stays in the system for a long time. So naturally Anthony always carries quinine."

"I never knew. He never told me."

"Is it likely Anthony would broadcast a weakness like that?"

"No, not likely at all." Despair washed over her again. "He'd never admit that he wasn't totally invulnerable." She closed her eyes. "He could have blacked out at any time last night."

Beau nodded. "But he didn't," he said quietly. "It didn't happen. Don't think about it."

"No, I won't think about it anymore." Thinking about it through those long hours last night had been enough for a lifetime, Dany thought. "Which hospital is he in, Beau?"

He hesitated. "He asked me not to tell you. He wants me to take you directly to Calgary so you can become accustomed to the ice in that new sports arena they've built. He said he'd join us in a week."

"I guess I should have expected that." She opened her eyes and there was only bleakness in their depths. "He'll appear on the scene when he's entirely strong again so no one will ever see the chinks in his armor. Not even me."

"It's not that he's afraid of appearing weak before you," Beau said, his face troubled. "He knows his weaknesses and strengths better than anyone I know. He just won't place you in a position where you'll feel obligated to help him." He opened his mouth as if to elaborate, but closed it again. "He has his reasons."

"And you know what they are, don't you, Beau?" Her lips twisted bitterly. "Well, I don't, and after last night I doubt if I ever will." She drew a shuddering breath. "I actually thought I had a chance." She wrapped her arms around herself. She couldn't get warm. She wondered if she would ever be warm again. "Funny, isn't it?"

"You do have a chance," Beau said gently. "So I know a little more about him than you do. We've gone through a hell of a lot together. Give him time, Dany."

"He could have died last night," she said fiercely, her eyes suddenly blazing. "He could have driven off the damn mountain and been killed. And all because he wouldn't let me help him. Because he wouldn't admit he needed someone . . . that he needed *me*! Do you know what that did to me? What I went through last night?"

"He was a sick man." The gold flecks in Beau's eyes were glowing softly. "Out of his head. You couldn't expect him to act naturally."

"He was at his weakest point last night. If he wouldn't take help then, he'll never take it." Her hands clenched on the silk of her sleeves. "I don't think I could stand to go through another night like last night. And I know I couldn't go through life with a man who refused to share the bad times as well as the good. I don't want to live only on the surface of Anthony's life, dammit!" She shrugged wearily. "I'm sorry, Beau. You can't help any of this and I don't have any right to cry on your shoulder." She turned toward the bedroom. "If you'll give me thirty minutes, I'll get dressed and packed. You might turn the generator off. It's in the utility shed out back."

"I'll do that," he said absently, watching her with troubled eyes as she disappeared into the bedroom.

It wasn't until they reached Briarcliff that Beau tried once again to pierce the wall that despair and bitterness had built. A troubled frown creased his forehead as he stood in the foyer and watched her start to climb the curving staircase.

"I don't like this, Dany," he said quietly. "I know that what Anthony did hurt you, but don't shut him out. I can practically see you turning hard before my eyes." His smile was sad. "There are enough of us out there with calluses on our souls."

She turned to look down at him. "Not you, Beau," she said softly. "You're everything that's warm and kind."

He shook his head. "You're seeing the man you want to see, Dany." His lips twisted. "I'm not really much different from the hellion I was seven years ago. I've grown up a little maybe, and I know who I am." His gaze met hers. For a moment his eyes flickered wild and golden, and she had a fleeting memory of Luisa's words. *Golden-eyed devil.* Then, that odd glint was gone and he was her steady, easygoing Beau again. "I can be just as ruthless and cynical as Anthony in my own way. You've just seen my charming big-brother side." He sketched a mocking bow. "A side no other lady has been honored to view, I might add."

"You're not going to convince me, you know." The smile faded from her face. "And you're not like Anthony. You wouldn't have done what he did last night. No one with any human feeling would have."

"Sometimes it's the people with the most intense emotions who make the greatest mistakes in human relations," Beau said quietly. "And who can be hurt the most. Don't try to put me on a pedestal, Dany." His lopsided grin was bittersweet. "It's always easy for me to be the charming southern gentleman because nothing has ever mattered a damn to me. I have a hunch that with Anthony it's been just the opposite. He cares so much that nothing's easy."

"Well, it's not easy for me either," she said wearily. "And I'm tired of fighting a losing battle. Anthony told me last night that he'd never need me. Never. And I believed him. I believe it even more today."

"Oh, hell!" Beau ran his hand through his hair. "Look, you two have got to get this straightened out. If I tell you the name of the hospital he's in, will you go see him and at least let him talk to you?"

"You'd run the risk of Anthony's ire?" she asked mockingly.

"I told you I've never been afraid of Anthony." His eyes met hers steadily. "I owe him, though, which is a very different thing, and I make it a habit always to pay my debts. Do you want the name of the hospital?"

She shook her head. "No, I don't think so. Anthony said it all last night." She tried to smile. "And I don't think I'm such a glutton for punishment that I want to hear it again."

"Dany—"

"No!" She tried to temper the sharpness in her voice. "I don't want to talk to him." She started to turn away and then swung back around. "I do want to talk to someone else, however. Would you see if you can find the number of Anthony's lawyer? I think his name is Donlevy or Donnely or something like that."

"Dunnely," Beau supplied. "Why do you want to speak to him?"

"We need to have a very important discussion before I leave for Calgary."

"We're supposed to leave at once," Beau said with a frown. "Can't it wait until we get back?"

"No. I doubt if we'll be coming back." She started back up the stairs. "I need to see him right away, but our business won't take very long. If you can get him out to Briarcliff today, we'll probably still be able to fly to Calgary this evening."

Chapter 8

"Beau's been looking for you for the last two hours," Marta said as soon as Dany entered the hotel suite to join her and Beau for dinner. "He didn't like the idea of you wandering all over Calgary by yourself." She frowned. "I didn't either. You never can tell what nutty terrorist group is going to try to use the games as a weapon to gain exposure for their cause. Remember Munich?"

"I try not to," Dany said with a shiver as she took off her coat. "It makes me feel a little sick when I do. Besides, I wasn't wandering around the city. After practice this morning I decided to go over to the slopes to see the downhill." Her smile became brilliant. "We won the gold, Marta. Isn't that terrific?"

"I know. I watched it on television." Marta's eyes were gentle as they rested on Dany's face. It was good to see her come alive again, Marta thought. In the week they'd been in Calgary she'd been so quiet, almost somber, that both she and Beau had been worried as hell. "He was wonderful, wasn't he?"

"Wonderful," Dany echoed as she crossed to the closet and reached in and took out a hanger. "We," she repeated dreamily. "I said *we* won the gold, and do you know, that's the way I felt when I stood there and watched them slowly raise the flag. Lord, I was proud." She hung the coat in the closet, shut the door, and leaned against it, her eyes still seeing the flag whipping in the breeze while "The Star-Spangled Banner" played triumphantly. "I cried," she said simply. "All of a sudden I realized that I wasn't only representing myself but my country. I know patriotism is considered old-fashioned, but by God, I *felt* patriotic." A little shadow crossed her face. "You know,

Anthony once said to me that when I won the gold, it would be a bribe to the whole world to love me. I think perhaps there might have been some truth in that at the time." She straightened and squared her shoulders. "But it's not true now. There are all sorts of reasons why I want to win the gold, but to use it as a bribe isn't one of them."

"He shouldn't have said that," Marta said gruffly.

"It hurt at the time; the truth often does." Dany dropped into the beige easy chair across from the couch where Marta was sitting. "But it made me think too. I've done a lot of thinking in the last week, and maybe a little growing up." She smiled sadly. "I thought I was so mature and wise before." She made a little face. "I was even a little smug." She held up her hand as Marta was about to protest. "I *was* smug. I was so self-centered that I couldn't see anything but my own point of view. I took yours and Beau's affection and support for granted. I resented being known as Anthony's Galatea but maybe I really needed a Pygmalion. I certainly wasn't a complete person on my own."

"And now you are?" Marta teased.

Dany shook her head. "No way. Give me another twenty or thirty years, and I just might make it."

"Well, if you want to have that twenty or thirty years, it would be wise to be a bit more careful about wandering around without Beau or me to run interference," Marta said dryly. "It's part of our job to keep you safe, and you're not letting us do it."

"Nonsense. Beau is my coach and you're my masseuse. Neither of you is responsible for my safety."

"No?" Marta lifted a skeptical brow. "Didn't it ever occur to you that a masseuse isn't required on a live-in basis? When Anthony hired me, he was much more interested in the fact that I was a security officer in the WACs than in my physical-therapy background. He made it very clear that my primary duty was going to be as bodyguard, not masseuse."

"No, it didn't occur to me." Dany's eyes had widened in shock. "I suppose, knowing Anthony, it should have. He's a great one for putting up protective barriers."

"You might consider that that particular barrier was built around you because he was genuinely worried about your safety," Marta said quietly. "You were in the public eye and the protégée of a very rich man. That can be a very dangerous position for a teenage girl to be placed in. He couldn't be with you, but he wanted to make sure you were as secure as if he were right there on the spot."

"Why didn't you tell me?"

"It wasn't necessary," Marta said calmly. "There wasn't any use worrying you about a situation that might never occur. And we were lucky. It never did occur. I could concentrate on being just your masseuse." She smiled. "And your friend, I hope."

"Oh, yes," Dany said, reaching out to clasp Marta's strong, square hand. "Above all, my friend, Marta." She blinked rapidly to keep back the tears. "I've been very lucky in the past six years—in more ways than one."

Marta cleared her throat. "And we'll work to keep it that way," she said briskly. "The four of us make a great team." She reached out for the phone on the end table beside the couch. "Now, suppose I phone Beau's room at the Olympic Village and let him know you're safe and sound. The last time he called he sounded pretty concerned."

The four of us, Dany mused. For a moment the pain was sharp and tearing. Not any longer. There would only be the three of them from now on. Then she lifted her chin and smiled with determined cheerfulness. "You'd better do that. We wouldn't want our Beau in a dither. It would definitely spoil his laid-back image."

She leaned back lazily in the chair and watched as Marta punched in the phone number and spoke into the receiver. It had been a good workout this morning, and she'd done better than she'd expected on the compulsory figures yesterday. She was going to be fine. All she had to do was live one day at a time, one moment at a time. Anthony had given her strength, and she could survive anything, even living without him.

"Dany."

Her attention flicked back to Marta, who was now replacing the receiver. She tensed as she saw the troubled, almost hesitant expression on Marta's face. "Beau said to tell you Anthony had called him between planes from Salt Lake City. That was nearly three hours ago and should have put him into the airport here about five thirty."

Dany cast a glance at her wristwatch. "It's almost six thirty now," she said, her voice calm and steady. How odd it was so steady when her heart was pounding so hard, she told herself. "He should be here at the hotel anytime." She stood up. "I'd better comb my hair and freshen up a little." She stood up and strode hurriedly across the sitting room toward the bathroom door. "Otherwise Anthony's going to think I'm a figment from his delirium. The wind on those slopes really tore me to pieces." She was speaking too fast. She bit her lower lip and tried to smile serenely. "Tell me when he—"

A knock sounded on the front door. A very firm, decisive knock.

"I don't think I'm going to have to tell you," Marta said dryly. "That's definitely an Anthony-type knock." She rose to her feet. "And I fully

intend to make myself scarce, so you can just answer the door yourself. I have an idea I'm going to
be in the way." As she passed Dany on the way to
the bedroom, she gave her a gentle push in the direction of the door. "Go on, Dany. Galatea had to
confront Pygmalion sometime. It may be easier
than you think."

Marta was right. For a moment she'd felt more
like Eliza Doolittle before her transformation, and
that wasn't to be tolerated. She moved determinedly to open the door.

Anthony looked thin and far paler than she'd
ever seen him in the dark business suit and
chesterfield overcoat. His skin was almost sallow
instead of the bronze she was accustomed to. Her
heart gave a queer little lurch. Had he been so ill
then?

There was nothing in the least weak or ill in his
demeanor, however. His silver-green eyes were
blazing, and the aura of vitality that surrounded
him was positively glowing. "Hello, Dany," he said
coolly as he stepped into the room and shut the
door behind him. "I see you made it back safely. It

wasn't very considerate of you to worry Beau and Marta by disappearing like that."

She stiffened. "I was perfectly all right," she protested. Then she drew a steadying breath. Anthony hadn't been in the room a moment and she was on the defensive. "You're right," she said quietly. "Next time I'll let them know where I'm going." She turned and walked to the center of the room. "Would you like to sit down? You don't appear any too well, Anthony. Perhaps you should have stayed in the hospital a little longer."

"I discharged myself three days ago," he said impatiently as he took off the charcoal-gray overcoat and tossed it carelessly on the couch. She felt a tremor of uneasiness. Anthony definitely wasn't his usual contained, orderly self, and it was obvious that the vitality she'd sensed was liberally laced with anger. "I've been tied up with business, hoping to clear the decks so I could get here for your short program."

"It's day after tomorrow," she said. "I did better than we expected on the compulsories." She rushed on hurriedly. "Nora Schmidt, the East German girl, is ahead of me, but I don't have as many points to make up as we thought I would. If I do well on the short program, I'll go into the long program in second place." *Slow down,* Dany told herself. *Don't let him see how upset you are.* "With the long program counting fifty percent of the total score, I've got a pretty good shot at first. You know the long program is always my forte."

"Yes, I know all that." Anthony's voice was very precise. "Now if you're quite finished imparting all the information Beau's kept me abreast of since you left Briarcliff, perhaps you'll be so kind as to explain the visit I received this morning from Dunnely."

"Only this morning?" Her hand reached out to trace the weave of the fabric on the high-backed chair she was standing beside. "I would have thought he'd get to you before that. He seemed like such an ultraefficient little man."

"He is," Anthony said crisply. "The only reason he didn't was that he assumed I'd be aware of what you were doing. It's not often a man is deeded a multimillion-dollar estate without his knowledge." His smile was mirthless. "Not to mention that charming promissory note you signed for two hundred thousand dollars. Dunnely was very impressed with your honesty and sense of responsibility. He couldn't understand why I was so angry."

"I told you I wouldn't accept Briarcliff," she said, looking down at the pattern her nail was tracing on the back of the chair. Lord, this was even more difficult than she'd imagined. The pain was growing with every second. "And I owe you the money you've invested in me over the years. It's probably much more now than those newspapers estimated. If you could have your accountant—"

"Be quiet!" His voice was so sharp it startled her, and she glanced up to see his eyes blazing with fury. "You sound like an accountant yourself, very cut and dried with all the loose ends neatly tied. Did you think I wouldn't realize what you were doing with that very expensive Dear John message you sent through Dunnely? It had a ringing note of finality." He drew a deep breath and was obviously trying to regain control. "You went to a great deal of trouble to make your gesture. Too bad it was all for nothing. Both of your very official documents went into the fire."

"You shouldn't have done that," she said steadily. "It only means I'll have to do them all over again."

"The hell you will!" His hands balled into fists. "I'm not accepting any walking papers from you, official or otherwise." His hands slowly un-clenched. "We're obviously going to have to talk it out. I gather from the hints Beau dropped that you were upset when I became ill. Look, I'm sorry if I caused you any inconvenience. I don't remember much about that night, but I realize that sickness isn't exactly attractive. I tried—"

"Attractive!" She was staring at him in disbe-lief. "What the hell do I care whether you were 'at-tractive' or not? You were sick. I wanted to help you. I would have done anything in the world to help you. What kind of self-centered woman do you think I am?"

His face softened. "You know what kind of woman I think you are. I've made that more than clear."

"Oh, yes, you've made that clear," she said, her voice shaking. "You 'love' me. You've learned to say the words now, but you don't really know what they mean. You proved that last week and you proved it again today."

"Because I wanted to spare you the drudgery and inconvenience of caring for a malaria victim?" he asked. "A fever case isn't all that easy or pretty."

"Who told you I wanted anything easy? All I asked is that you share with me. I wanted to know the bad times as well as the good. You couldn't understand that, could you, Anthony? You thought I'd be satisfied just coasting along and letting you take all the responsibility and the hard knocks just as you've always done." Her voice was suddenly fierce. "You could have *died* that night. If you'd been dangling from the side of that damn mountain and I'd held out my hand to help, you'd probably have refused to accept it. You'd rather have me go through the hell of waiting and wondering if I was ever going to see you again." Her dark eyes were blazing now. "Well, I'm not going to stand by and let you do it to me again. Not ever. You almost destroyed me that night. You told me you didn't need me and never would. Okay, I'll go along with that, but I can't live in the same little insular cocoon you do. I'll just have to learn not to need you too." She paused. "And for me that also means learning not to love you."

"So we're back to square one," he said coolly. "I'm being shown the door. You know, of course, that I'm not going to accept that. I told you that from now on you were going to belong to me. Nothing you've said has changed that." His lips twisted in a bitter smile. "I'm afraid I don't have your powers of adaptability. I can't stop loving you because it hurts me or is best for me. It just goes on." He abruptly stepped forward, his hands grasping her shoulders. "And I think it's going to go on for you too. Even if you can stop caring for me, you're going to want me." He suddenly pulled her close to the warmth of his body and smiled mockingly as he saw the shiver of response that went through her. "See? That insurance I took out is paying dividends. You're going to lie awake at night and remember all the things we did together, and you're going to want to do them again." His hand dropped to encircle her breast, lifting and toying with its soft weight through the cashmere sweater. "You're going to ache and throb until I'm back beside you in that bed." His eyes held hers with mesmerizing intensity. "I'd be willing to wager you've already been doing that—just as I have, Dany." The color flooded her cheeks and there was a trace of a bittersweet satisfaction in his smile. "I thought so."

"I'll get over it," she said desperately.

He shook his head. "No, you won't. For the simple reason that I'm not going to let you. Whenever you turn around, I'll be there reminding you. I'm going to be the shadow behind you and the nemesis in front of you. You'll be back in my bed within a month."

"No," she whispered. "I'm stronger than that."

"In a battle against anyone else perhaps," he said, his silver-green eyes glacier-cold. His hand squeezed her breast gently and she felt liquid fire begin to smolder in the pit of her stomach. "I think you'll find it an entirely different matter when it comes to fighting yourself." His hands fell away from her and he stepped back. "It's too late to back away from me now, Dany. I'll just come after you. For the rest of your life I'll be either beside you or behind you. Take your pick." He picked up his coat from the couch and draped it over his arm. "Don't worry. I'm not going to harass you while we're in Calgary. I won't even try to see you until the competition is over." He turned toward the door. "I want all your concentration on your work. I can wait. I've become very good at that over the years."

"It won't do you any good," Dany said despairingly.

"I think it will." He turned at the door, and for a moment his eyes were no longer cool but naked and raw with pain. "And you're wrong. If you held out your hand to save me from a precipice, I'd take it in a minute. I wouldn't let even death separate us now."

The competitor from East Germany raised her leg in a camel spin with a precise grace that was a miracle of strength and coordination. "She's almost swanlike," Dany whispered to Beau from where they stood on the sidelines observing Nora Schmidt's short program. "And she's very strong too. I noticed that in Brussels last year when she placed third in the Worlds. Her long program should be even better than her short."

"She's not so great," Marta sniffed from beside her. "Her legs are too long. She looks like a giraffe."

"You said Margie Brandon looked like a cow on ice," Dany said affectionately. "We're rapidly acquiring a menagerie."

"Well, I was right," Marta said with satisfaction. "You noticed that Brandon only placed fourteenth in the compulsories."

"Schmidt's program's been practically faultless," Beau said. His eyes were narrowed on the dark-haired skater as she ended the program with a beautifully executed spin. "That classical style combined with her technical precision will almost certainly keep her in first. I was hoping she'd screw up so you'd have a chance of taking over first right away. It would take a hell of a lot of pressure off you."

Dany shrugged. "We're in no worse shape than we thought we'd be." She made a wry face. "That is, we won't be if *I* don't screw up." She straightened the sky-blue chiffon of her costume. "I'm up next, aren't I?"

"Right after Schmidt's second set of scores come up," Beau drawled. "And you won't screw up. You and Scarlett are both survivors, remember?"

"How could I forget?" she said lightly, then impulsively asked the question she'd been avoiding thinking about all afternoon. "Is Anthony here, Beau?"

He didn't answer for a moment. "He's here," he finally said quietly. "He decided not to come back to the dressing room. He's in a front row box across the arena. Is it going to bother you to know that?"

"No, it won't bother me," she said with a reassuring smile. She carefully kept her gaze from searching the arena. She didn't want to know exactly where Anthony was, but she'd been telling the truth when she'd said Anthony's presence didn't disturb her. Even if all other aspects of their relationship had changed, she knew that one hadn't. She knew he'd be giving her silent support, willing her to succeed, willing her to be all she could be. She felt her spirits lift just at the thought. "It can only help."

She heard the burst of applause from the audience as the East German girl's second set of scores came up. "She's tied up first, sugar," Beau said as he gave her a little push onto the ice. "Now, go bring home second."

Her short program had been planned as spirited, vigorous, and sparkling with a virtual fireworks display of technical skill and intricate footwork. She could feel the audience with her all the way as she began to have fun with it. Not for her the stately classics. She was more the mischievous little girl showing off for the grown-ups. Her piquant face was alive with a joie de vivre as lively as the performance itself as the audience began to clap with the tempo of the music. She was still wishing it could go on forever when the final, beautifully blurred sit-spin came much too soon.

She stood in the middle of the rink, a little breathless, her cheeks flushed and her dark eyes shining as she raised her hand in acknowledgement of the storm of applause. Now, wrapped in the sweetness of the moment, she could afford to search the ringside boxes for Anthony.

There he was, sitting quietly, not applauding as the rest of the crowd was doing. But, oh, his face! Pride, love, and an odd sadness combined with an intensity that took her breath away and caused an aching tenderness to replace the euphoria she'd been feeling. She looked away hurriedly and skated back to where Beau and Marta were waiting.

Beau gave her a light kiss on the end of her nose. "You were as smooth as a mint julep on a hot summer day." His gaze was fixed on the scoreboard across the rink. "There are the technical marks: all good except for East Germany. He gave you a five point five." His lips tightened. "He won't dare do that on the artistic. The bias would be too obvious."

"Besides, the crowd would lynch him," Marta said grimly. "And I'll be the one yanking the rope."

Dany held Beau's arm for balance as she put on her blade guards, her eyes fixed anxiously on the board. "Will it be enough, Beau?" She moistened her lips nervously. "That five point five is going to drag the composite score down so much."

Beau didn't answer, his tense gaze on the board.

Then the scores began to flicker on one by one, and the crowd roared its approval. 5.8, 5.9, 5.9, 5.9 . . .

Beau picked her up and whirled her in an exuberant circle. "You did it! Nothing lower than a five point eight except East Germany, and even that bastard gave you a five point seven! That makes you a shoo-in for the number two spot when you go into the long program. We're halfway home!"

Dany felt ten feet tall. No, fifty feet tall, and skating on clouds instead of ice as Beau let her down and Marta launched herself at her and enfolded her in an ecstatic bear hug. She'd done it! The crowd was applauding wildly, and Beau and Marta were hugging and congratulating her with all the affection and love in the world. Everything was wonderful!

She wasn't sure if it was by accident or design that her gaze alighted on Anthony's box across the arena. Lord, he looked so alone. She was surrounded by more love and adulation than ever before in her life, and he should have been sharing it. It was wrong to have him sitting half an arena away, half a world away, in that chilly isolation. She impulsively started to speak, to ask Beau to go after him and bring him into their warm circle.

Then she saw him rise gracefully to his feet and leave the box. His back was straight and indomitable and the set of his shoulders almost arrogantly proud. In less than a minute she lost sight of him in the crowd.

"Dany?" Beau's eyes glowed softly with sympathy. "Are you okay?"

Why was she feeling this crushing disappointment? Anthony wouldn't have wanted to share their heady triumph anyway. Nothing had changed since their scene in the hotel suite the day before yesterday.

"Of course I am," she said with a determined

smile. "And I'll be even better three days from now when I go for the gold." She linked her arms through Beau's and Marta's. "Come on, I've got that TV interview to get through, and then we're going to celebrate."

Chapter 9

"How did you sleep last night?" Beau asked as he dropped down in his favorite position, straddling the straight-backed chair across from the bench where she was sitting and resting his arms on the back. "Any nerves?"

She shook her head. "A few, but nothing major." She put her skates in the bag, zipped it up, and set it on the dressing-room bench beside her. "I slept very well from ten o'clock on."

"And the workout went smooth as glass this morning." He frowned. "Almost too well. You know what they say about a bad dress rehearsal making a hit on opening night. I don't want you making your mistakes tonight in the performance." Then his face cleared and he shook his head ruefully. "Just listen to me! *I'm* the one who has the nerves."

Her dark eyes were twinkling. "If it will make you feel any better, I'll go back on the ice and try to fall down a couple of times."

"Don't you dare. With my luck you'd probably break something and I'd be accused of ruining your brilliant career."

Her face softened. "I'd never do that. You've worked like a demon to get me to this point. The only reason I have a chance at that brilliant career is because of all the support you've given me over the years. Marta was right when she said we make a great team." She leaned forward to squeeze his arm. "I guess after tonight that team will just have to concentrate on new fields to conquer."

He covered her hand with his own. "We did make a good team." He paused and seemed to hesitate. "I didn't mean to go into this until after the competition, but I think you should know I won't be around after next week." At her startled exclamation he went on quickly. "You won't need me.

No matter how tonight goes, you'll have all the ice shows clamoring for you. You have star quality, Dany."

"I'll always need you." First Anthony and now Beau, she thought. She was going to lose them both. "We're a team."

He shrugged restlessly. "Well, the truth is, I've always been a loner. I've never pulled well in harness." He smiled. "I consider it something of a miracle to have made it this long without kicking over the traces." His hand tightened on hers. "I told you once I wasn't the steady, upright paragon you thought me."

"But you are," she protested. "You've always been—"

"And sometimes it's almost driven me crazy," he interrupted. For a moment she saw once again that wild golden gleam in the depths of his eyes. "I'm not a responsible heavyweight like Anthony. I wouldn't want to be. I *like* to raise hell and do what I damn well please."

"You've been exceptionally responsible for the past six years."

"I owed a debt," he said simply. "The thing

Anthony wanted most in the world was the gold for you. I knew I couldn't give him anything else. It had to be the gold."

"So you gave him six years of your life. In a job you didn't want to do." She was gazing at him in wonder. "That's unbelievable, Beau. It's like something from the Old Testament."

"It wasn't all that rough," he said. "I found playing big brother to a fourteen-year-old easier than I thought." He reached out to touch the tip of her nose teasingly in the gesture she knew so well. "Because I grew to like and admire that teenager very much. Before I took on this job, the only family I'd ever known was a battery of lawyers and executors. In a way you, Marta, and Anthony have been my family."

"But not a close-enough tie to keep you here," Dany said sadly.

"Well, every family has its black sheep," he said with a lopsided grin. "You haven't seen the last of me. Every now and then, like any prodigal, I'll be dropping in for my dinner of fatted calf."

"You'll get it," she said huskily. "Anytime,

Beau." She cleared her throat. "What are you going to do now? Go back to the ice show?"

He shook his head. "I was ready to hang up my skates seven years ago when I left the clinic. I've never cared enough about anything to stick to it for an indefinite period. It was fun for a while, and I was young enough to enjoy all the show-biz glamor and groupies throwing themselves into my bed." His eyes twinkled mischievously. "I particularly enjoyed that fringe benefit."

"From what I hear, that benefit didn't end when you left the show," Dany said dryly.

His lips twisted cynically. "Most women think a checkbook glitters just as much as a spotlight." He inclined his head mockingly. "Not to mention my irresistible physique and charisma."

"By all means, let's do mention both of those attributes," Dany said lightly. "So what's ahead, Beau?"

"I thought I'd drift around the world a bit. I'm looking at a schooner for sale down in Miami. I may get a crew together and sail around the coast of South America."

"A sailing ship?" Dany asked blankly. "That's

certainly a change of lifestyle with a vengeance. Why South America?"

"I'm tired of all this ice," Beau drawled, making a face. "I'm going to let the tropical sun sink into these weary old bones."

"And let a multitude of tropical señoritas sink into your bunk?" Dany asked, amused.

"That thought did occur to me." The creases in the corners of his eyes deepened as he grinned. "After all, if I'm giving up skating, I have to substitute some sport to keep in shape."

She chuckled. "You're impossible."

"That's what I've been trying to tell you." Beau's face was suddenly grave. "I don't belong to anyone or anywhere. I'm not the stuff stability is made of like you and Anthony."

Her smile faded. "Well, I can't argue with you in Anthony's case at least," she said tightly. "There's no one as unchangeable as Anthony."

He studied her taut, strained face for a long moment before he slowly shook his head. "I can't leave things like this, you know," he said quietly. "I don't give a damn about most people, but I'm not about to go sailing off into the sunset while you and Anthony are hurting each other like this."

"Then you may be sticking around for quite a while," she said, trying to smile.

"The hell I will," he said bluntly. "I'm much too selfish for that. The gloves are now officially off."

"You sound very grim."

"That's the way I feel." He released her hand. "I've been zooming around in a discreet holding pattern, waiting and watching for you and Anthony to straighten out your problems. For two intelligent people you haven't done at all well."

"Some problems aren't that easy to straighten out," she said defensively.

"Bull," he said succinctly. "You're talking to me, remember? I've watched you turn yourself from a talented junior into a world-class Olympic contender by sheer force of will and hard work. Don't tell me if you bent that same determination toward resolving your differences with Anthony that you couldn't do it."

"I'm not the only one involved. Anthony—"

"Anthony isn't willing to make concessions so that the world will be exactly the way you want it to be," he said caustically. "I realize that's a terrible crime."

Her eyes widened in shock. Beau had never spoken to her with such brutality before. "You know what happened that night at the lodge."

"I know that Anthony fell out of that cozy little niche you created for him. I told you building pedestals was a dangerous thing to do." He paused. "But no more than making judgments. Who the hell gave you the right to do that? So Anthony backslid and gave you a bad time. How many bad times have you had in your life, for God's sake? Not many, thanks to Anthony."

"Why are you acting like this?" she whispered, her eyes bright with tears. "It's not like you."

"Another niche? I don't fit in them any more comfortably than Anthony." Then, as his eyes met hers, he said wearily, "For Pete's sake, stop looking at me as if I were a murderer. I know I don't have any right to preach. I grew up with the same silver spoon you did, but I've gotten to the point when I at least try to understand."

"Understand what?" she asked shakily.

"Anthony," he answered. Beau ran his hand

through his hair distractedly. "Look, I'm going to break Anthony's confidence." He scowled. "It had better help, dammit." His gaze was fixed absently on his folded arms on the back of the chair. "It's not something Anthony's likely to tell you. It was pretty painful for him letting it out to me." His lips twisted grimly. "The only reason he did was that I was practically suicidal at the time. It was just before I entered the clinic. I was pretty sick with myself and my own weakness. You have no idea of the self-disgust alcoholism can generate. I know I told you I would have preferred to see my problem as a romantic weakness. That was bull. It's hard to drop my guard even with you and admit how I hated the idea of being so helpless and uncontrolled." He glanced up, his face dark with memories.

"Anthony convinced me that I wasn't weak, that I was a strong man with an illness. You can imagine what that did for my self-respect. I felt clean again. Do you know how he convinced me? He said he knew what weakness was and he'd recognize it if he saw it." He paused. "And he told me about his father."

"His father?"

"I gathered his mother either died or deserted them before Anthony could remember her. There was only his father." His voice became bitter. "With a father like his, that was more than enough. He was into booze, pills, and self-pity—in that order. He leaned on anyone or anything and, as Anthony was the closest, it was mostly him. He doesn't remember his father ever having a job. Anthony grew up on welfare. Do you realize how that kind of public dependence would grate on a kid like Anthony?"

"Yes," Dany said. To a proud, independent spirit like Anthony's it would have been barely tolerable. "I realize that."

"He had a job after school at the neighborhood ice rink from the time he was seven, first running errands and then as a monitor. He didn't say, but I doubt if he was able to keep any of the money he earned. He did mention his father would often go on crying jags and tell Anthony over and over how grateful he was for all Anthony's help and how much he needed him."

"Oh, God, no." How could a child stand that

kind of pressure? He must never have been allowed even a vestige of childhood.

"Pretty, isn't it?" Beau said ironically. "And do you know what Anthony said was the worst part of the situation? He couldn't stop loving his father. If he hadn't loved him, he might have been able to refuse to let his father use him and might have made him pull himself together. He had to stand by and watch his father disintegrate as a human being because of a moral fiber as brittle as chalk. All Anthony could give him was the support that only made him lean harder." He drew a deep breath. "He died when Anthony was twelve, right after Dynathe appeared on the scene. It's just as well, since from what I hear of Samuel Dynathe, he wouldn't have thought twice about slipping an arsenic mickey to anyone who got in his way."

Anthony had gone from crushing dependence to equally crushing ruthlessness, Dany thought. He'd never had a chance. It's a wonder he hadn't become a callous monster. Instead, through his own efforts, he'd developed into a man to respect and admire.

"Do you understand why he can't stand the thought of dependence in himself or anyone else?" Beau asked soberly. "He must see ghosts whenever the word is mentioned. Why do you think he fostered and guarded that strength and independence in you so fiercely? Perhaps he was a little overzealous, but you can't really blame him." He paused. "Did you know he's not planning on being at the competition tonight?"

"He's not?" Dany's eyes widened. "But it's everything we've been working for. He's got to be there!"

"If you remember, he wasn't at the Worlds or the United States Championships. He's only present at the minor competitions. Does that form any pattern for you?"

"It's beginning to," she said slowly. "But why don't you spell it out?"

"Anyone would have to be crazy to believe he wouldn't want to be with you at important times like those. I think it may have meant almost as much to him as to you. The only explanation possible was that he thought he might weaken you by having you develop a reliance on him." His eyes steadily met hers. "And you'll have to admit, there was a point when you would have formed an emotional dependence if he'd allowed it. He didn't want to cheat you of the knowledge that any victory was totally yours. Even if it meant he couldn't share it with you."

She had a sudden painful memory of Anthony sitting alone and isolated in the box across the arena. How many other times had he shut himself away from warmth and togetherness for her sake?

"That idiot," she said huskily, blinking rapidly to keep back the tears. "God, he's an idiot. Maybe there was a time when I was in danger of losing a little of my independence, but there wasn't any need for him to do that."

"He thought there was," Beau said quietly. "He wanted what he thought was best for you. What his own experience dictated was best for you. He may have been mistaken, but you can't accuse him of not caring. Like I told you, Anthony's problem is that he cares too much."

"I can see that." She felt an aching tenderness that was so powerful, it seemed to encompass her whole world. She loved him. Why hadn't she realized that that was the only clear, shining truth that mattered? Beau was right; she'd been so concerned with her own pain, she'd been blind to everything else. She felt a sudden rush of panic. What if she'd lost Anthony through her own stupidity? "*I'm* the one who's been the idiot. Why the hell didn't you tell me, Beau?"

"I thought you'd reach that conclusion yourself," he drawled. "You probably would have if I hadn't gotten impatient and decided to accelerate the process."

"I hope you're right." She stood up and reached for her polo coat on the bench beside her. "I'd hate to think that I'd have remained that pigheaded indefinitely."

"Where are you going?"

"Where do you think?" she asked as she slipped on the coat and belted it around her waist. "To the hotel to see Anthony." She bit her lip worriedly. "You don't suppose he's left Calgary?"

Beau shook his head. "I talked to him last night, and he said he'd see me tonight after the long program." He smiled gently as he saw her face light up. "Don't get too excited, sugar. Anthony is a very difficult man, and you still have a lot of differences to iron out."

"Understanding can go a long way in that direction," she said serenely. "And from now on I'm going to make damn sure I never let him leave my sight with a misunderstanding looming on the horizon."

"You sound very determined." Beau's lips were twitching. "Have I created a monster?"

She leaned down to brush her lips on his cheek. "You've created an Olympic competitor who will be grateful to you for the rest of her life." She turned to the door. "And who's going to channel all that drive and force of will you credit me with toward acquiring an entirely different kind of prize."

She paused for a moment outside the door of Anthony's suite and tried to steady her breathing and control the sudden butterflies in the pit of her stomach. This was Anthony, for heaven's sake, the man she wanted to be a part of her. He'd said he loved her and couldn't change that fact, only a few days ago. All she had to do was mend the breach and try to reach an understanding with him. She shook her head ruefully at the way she'd minimized the most potentially important and difficult task of her life. What could she say that would accomplish that goal when her mind had suddenly gone blank with nervousness? Oh, well, it had to be done, and she'd find a way of doing it. She knocked firmly on the door.

When Anthony opened the door, the way she found was very simple and straightforward and self-explanatory. She flowed into his arms and kissed him with all the love and tenderness that was welling up inside her like a bubbling spring. She felt him stiffen against her. Then his arms went around her, and the kiss turned to passion as he crushed her to him with bruising force.

She felt as if she were going up in flames as his tongue entered and probed and his body hardened with the same desire that was softening her own. It had been so long. Her body had grown so used to the magical physical intimacy during those two weeks with him. Now he was here, pressed against her with a need as deep as her own. In a moment he'd move away and then take her to the bed-room, his hands moving over her with his usual deftness as he took off. . . .

"No!" What was she thinking about? This wasn't why she'd come here. She tore her lips from his, her hands pushing at his chest. "Let me go!"

"Why?" he muttered, his lips covering hers again in a kiss as meltingly explosive as the first. "This is what you want. I can feel it." He arched her up against him. "You have too many clothes on." One hand untied the belt of the polo coat, pushed it open, and brought her into the cradle of his hips. She inhaled sharply and forgot for a moment that this wasn't her prime motivation for coming to him. He was so aroused, as ready for her as she was for him.

Unconsciously she nestled closer, and she could hear the almost guttural satisfaction in his voice. "That's better." His hands were rapidly unbutton-ing her blouse. "Just a little longer and we'll both be where we want to be. I don't think I've slept for more than a few hours at a time since I left the lodge. I'd wake up and reach for you and you wouldn't be there." His hand closed on her breast, covered only by the lacy bra, and its warmth came as a tiny shock. "And I'd lie there wanting you and fantasizing all the things I was going to do to you once you were back where you belonged. Remember that afternoon when I—"

"No, please . . . I don't want this." Then when he looked up in patent disbelief, she continued hurriedly. "Well, I do, but not right now." As he continued to stare at her, her brow knotted in confusion. No wonder he was looking at her like that. Her breast was swelling and nestling into his palm as if it had come home. "What I mean is that I think we should talk instead."

"No way." His voice was suddenly harsh. "You came here because you want me just the way I want you. I'd be a fool if I didn't consolidate my position before I let you start verbally tearing our relationship apart again." His lips twisted. "I'll salvage whatever I can and worry about the rest later."

That hint of bitterness brought her rudely down to earth. He obviously believed she'd come to him for that physical assuagement he'd said was his most potent weapon. If she gave in to that need now, he'd never be sure that wasn't the primary factor that brought her to him. She couldn't permit that. Everything about their life together from now on must be clear and shining and based on a foundation of trust and understanding.

"That's why I'm here," she said gently. "I decided I had some salvaging to do too." Suddenly her eyes were dancing. "But I'll have to ask you to remove your hand. I'm finding it very hard to concentrate."

His hand didn't move from its position, but his eyes narrowed searchingly on her face. "You seem to be in considerably brighter spirits than the last time we had a discussion," he said warily. "Am I to assume you've decided I'm to be tentatively reinstated in your affections?"

"There's nothing tentative about it," she told him with a serene smile. "Unless you want it that way." She reached up and firmly removed his hand from her breast. "But I warn you that if you opt for that, I'm going to do everything I can to change your mind. I wouldn't be above using a little sexual blackmail myself if you drive me to it."

She was buttoning up her blouse with hands that were shaking slightly. "I'm through with ifs, ands, or buts. I think it's time we got rid of all those uncertainties and qualifications." She drew a deep breath. "Will you marry me, Anthony?"

"What?" His eyes widened in shock before they narrowed with sudden suspicion. "Why? Are you pregnant, Dany?" A worried frown darkened his face. "I suppose I should have expected it. I didn't protect you half the time we were together. I meant to, but when I'm making love to you I go a little crazy. God, I'm sor—"

She put her hand over his lips. "I'm not pregnant," she said firmly. "And even if I were, I wouldn't come running to you in panic." She removed her hand. "It would have been just as much my responsibility as yours, and I'd have accepted the consequences and dealt with it on my own."

He scowled. "In the currently approved modern fashion, I assume. There won't be any abortions for my child, Dany."

"I told you there wasn't a child," she said in loving exasperation. "But if there were, I'm afraid

I'd handle it in a shockingly old-fashioned and traditional manner. I'd have your baby and love and cherish it as long as I lived. Now will you forget about our nonexistent offspring and pay attention to me? I've just asked you a very important question."

"But you still didn't answer mine," he said slowly. "If you're not pregnant, why are you suddenly suing for my heart and hand?" His lips curved in a cynical smile. "If I recall, I was considered one of the lowly untouchables only a few days ago."

She broke away from him and backed away. She couldn't think when he was so close. He was so beautiful, she thought tenderly. The weight he'd lost only threw that fascinating bone structure into bolder prominence. The dark green of his collarless shirt made his eyes glow pale and jewel-like in contrast. "I'm afraid I'm shockingly old-fashioned and traditional about you too," she said softly. "I want to love and cherish you for the rest of my life in the same way."

For an instant he had an odd, stunned expression on his face as if she'd struck him. Then the wariness was back. "I haven't noticed I've suddenly sprouted wings. How have I earned all this boundless devotion?"

"You began fourteen years ago," she said simply. "You gave me your love and your loyalty and your support every moment of every day from then until today. Beau tells me he always pays his debts. Well, so do I. It's about time I began to return all you've given me. Will you marry me and let me try, Anthony?"

"Beau?" His tone had suddenly sharpened. "Dammit, did Beau bulldoze you into coming here?" He uttered a soft but still audible and quite obscene curse. "Well, you can turn around and go out the way you came in. He doesn't owe me a blasted thing, and you certainly don't. Even if he convinced you it was your duty to give me ano—"

"Anthony, shut up!" she said clearly and with utmost precision. "I have a few things to clear up in that muddled psyche of yours, and I'd appreciate it if you'd give me the opportunity." She ignored his expression of amazement tinged with indignation and proceeded with composure. "First, we'll take up the matter of gratitude. I have been grateful to you, I am grateful to you, I shall be grateful to you. I believe that about covers all the tenses. So don't say anything more about how you won't accept it because you don't have any choice. Just because your father—"

"My father!" he interrupted, his lips tightening grimly. "Beau *has* been busy. No wonder you're practically oozing pity and loving-kindness. I won't let you—"

"I'm obviously going to have to gag you," she said with a rueful sigh. "Dear heaven, how could I possibly pity you? You're one of the strongest and most dynamic men I've ever known. I might have pitied that little boy who had the whole damn world against him, but not you. Not the man you are now. And Beau wouldn't have had to tell me about him if you'd only told me yourself." Her voice deepened with intensity. "Couldn't you see I *needed* to know?"

"It doesn't change anything. It's all past history."

"The study of history is meant to make you understand the present," she said softly. "Our present. Understanding is the name of the game when it comes to relationships. I'd never have been so hurt and helpless that night at the lodge if I'd known why you were behaving as you were. I'd have been more secure." She suddenly grinned impishly. "Secure enough to have bashed you on the head with a lamp before I'd have let you drive off down that damn mountain."

"Perhaps I'd be safer if you were a little less secure," he said dryly. For the first time since she'd entered the suite there was a little smile tugging at the corners of his lips. "In your case it appears to breed violent tendencies."

"Too late," she said with an airy wave of her hand. "You see before you an eminently secure and understanding woman. Don't worry, you'll get used to it in time."

"How very comforting." There was a thread of tenderness in his voice. "I'll have to remember that when the threatened bash on the head becomes a reality."

"It won't ever come to that." Her dark eyes were glowing softly. "Not if you hold out your hand to me and say, 'Dany, I need you.' And you're going to do that someday. It doesn't have to be today or tomorrow. I can wait. I can wait for the next fifty years if I have to. Because you do need me, just as I need you."

His expression was troubled. "I love you. Isn't that enough for you?"

She shook her head. "No, it's not enough. Somewhere along the way you got the wrong idea about what needing someone meant. You thought it would always make you weak and dependent on that person. Well, it's not like that always. Sometimes it does just the opposite and makes you stronger instead." Her expression was almost luminous. "When you love someone, it's the most beautifully natural thing in the world to need that person to complete you, to enrich you and make you soar." Her eyes met his serenely. "I can live without you, Anthony. Beau called me a survivor and I *will* survive. I'll go into that competition tonight and I'll do my damnedest to win the gold. I *intend* to win it. I'm not depending on you to help me or fight any of my battles for me. I'll fight them and win them myself. But that doesn't mean I won't always need you to stand beside me and support me." Her voice was so soft now, it was almost a whisper. "You're the ice beneath my skates and the wind beneath my wings. You're my lover and my friend. There's no shame in needing someone like that. Someday you'll come to understand that."

He took an impulsive step forward. "Dany . . ."

She backed away and shook her head. She was blinking furiously to keep back the tears. "No, don't touch me," she said huskily. "I think if you did, I'd break into a million pieces, and I can't do that. Not if I want to keep intact that control you instilled in me all these years." Her lips were trembling a little as she smiled. "Heaven knows, I'm going to need every bit of it tonight." She turned away. "I'd better get out of here. I've said what I wanted to say."

His voice was deep and velvet-gentle behind her. "Stay, Dany. I want to hold you."

She paused with her hand on the doorknob. "I want that too," she said quietly. She looked over her shoulder. "Beau said you weren't planning on coming to the competition tonight."

He hesitated and then slowly shook his head. "No."

"I want you to come. I want you beside me sharing my victory or my defeat. It's only fair that you know that." Her voice was grave. "But I also want it to be entirely your own decision. I want you to take the time to think over what I've said. If I stayed now, we'd probably end up in bed and that might influence you." She smiled mistily. "I wouldn't want to be accused of offering a bribe. I don't do that anymore." She opened the door. "I'll understand if you're not there. It won't change the way I love you, and I'll be right here knocking on your door after I leave the arena tonight."

The door closed softly behind her.

Chapter 10

"Just sit down at that table and be still."
Marta's hands on her shoulders firmly reinforced
the order, and Dany found herself once more staring into the brilliantly lit mirror. "You're not quite
finished."

"Look, my makeup is perfect," Dany said impatiently. "My bun is a work of art, and you've
sprayed it so heavily, it would take a full-scale
hurricane to budge it. Will you please let me out of
here? I want to get out front and see how Schmidt
is doing."

"In a minute," Marta said calmly, opening
the drawer of the makeup table. "Watching her

performance isn't going to change anything one way or the other. It might even make you more nervous." She pulled out a long, black leather jewelry box. "If that's possible. You're so flushed, I didn't have to use any rouge at all, and your eyes are blazing as if you have a fever." She suddenly frowned. "You don't, do you?"

"No, I feel great." Dany made a face at Marta's reflection in the mirror. "Or I would if you'd just let me join Beau out front." Her gaze went to the jeweler's box in Marta's hands. "What's that? You know I don't wear jewelry when I'm performing. It bothers me."

"I don't think this will." Marta opened the box. "It was delivered to the sports arena tonight by special messenger. Attached was a note from the jeweler saying that Mr. Malik had special-ordered it to go with your costume." She was looking admiringly into the black velvet-lined case. "It will do that all right. I was thinking Anthony had made a mistake to have ordered such a plain design for that little bit of nothing you're wearing, but this will make you into a fairy princess."

She held up a silver chain so slender and

exquisitely fragile that it looked as if it had been woven by fairies. Intersticed so closely on the chain that there appeared to be no separation were beautifully cut diamonds that shimmered under the lights as if they were alive. Each was mounted in a star setting.

"They're so beautiful," Dany whispered. "They can't be real, can they?"

"They're real, all right," Marta said dryly. "There was a security guard accompanying the messenger." She was swiftly winding the gorgeous chain around the base of the bun on the top of Dany's head, using special clips to fasten it securely in place.

As Marta said, it was just the right touch. Her white tulle costume was elegantly simple. Its long sleeves, off-the-shoulder neckline, and tight bodice were completely unadorned. Only the diaphanous short skirt that moved and flared with every movement kept it from looking almost medieval. Her smooth golden shoulders and throat rose proudly from the stark white in glowing contrast, and now the chain of diamonds encircling the rich auburn of her hair gave her costume a regal dignity.

"A crown of stars," Marta said as she stepped back and gazed critically at Dany's reflection in the mirror. "That will catch those judges' eyes. Do you think that's what Anthony had in mind? Sort of a subliminal nudge in the right direction?"

"Perhaps," Dany murmured, gazing unseeingly into the mirror. She had a fleeting memory of Anthony's enigmatic words that afternoon in the hot tub. "But somehow I don't think so."

"Well, it's very effective anyway." Marta's strong, gentle hands closed on her shoulders in an affectionate little squeeze. "You're gorgeous tonight, Dany. You'll knock those judges on their collective tushes."

"Just so I don't end up on mine," Dany said lightly as she reached up to pat Marta's left hand resting on her shoulder. "*Now* can I go and check out the competition?"

"You don't have any," Marta said gruffly as she stepped back and helped Dany to her feet. "You just remember that when you're out there on the ice."

"I'll remember," Dany said, leaning forward to press a light kiss on Marta's cheek. "Are you coming?"

"In a minute. I want to straighten up here first. I'll be there before it's time for you to go on."

Dany nodded. "I'll see you there." She opened the door and walked swiftly down the long, empty corridor toward the door that opened onto the rink itself. Naturally it was empty, Dany thought wryly. Everyone was watching with bated breath while Schmidt made her try for the gold. Her music, the overture to *Swan Lake,* was just ending. A rather obvious choice considering her classical style, Dany thought, but the German girl was probably skating it superlatively. Her palms suddenly felt moist and clammy, and she wiped them on the soft tulle of her skirt. She mustn't let that thought shake her. Of course, Schmidt was skating superbly, but so would she.

She was almost at the door now, her feet moving with a clumping awkwardness in their skate guards. She always felt like a beached mermaid when she wore blade protectors. She opened the door and now the music was much louder. The corridor between the tiers of seats was crowded with skaters, coaches, and the television cameramen. She stepped carefully over several long rubber cords attached to those TV cameras and sighed with relief as she spotted Beau's bronze hair just ahead and to the left, his gaze intent on the scoreboard across the arena.

She slipped her arm through his. "Has she finished?" she whispered. "How did she do?"

"Good," Beau said grimly. "Damn good. Her technical scores were all five point nine except for Canada. He gave her a five eight." The board suddenly flickered into motion again. Beau's lips pursed in a soundless whistle. "Not as good in artistic impression, but still excellent. You're going to have to go all the way to knock her out of first." He glanced down at her. "You always did like a challenge."

"I could have done without such a big one at the moment." Dany moistened her lips nervously. "Nothing like going into the game knowing the other player is holding the aces."

"Not aces, Dany. Maybe a few kings." The

voice behind her was deep and velvet-soft. "You're the one who holds the aces."

Anthony.

She whirled around, her heart leaping with wild, heady joy. Oh, dear heaven, Anthony!

He was standing there, wearing his gray chesterfield overcoat, his hands jammed into the pockets, his dark hair slightly ruffled. "I've been drumming that philosophy into you for the past fourteen years. I thought you'd have learned by now. You're the best damn skater in the world. All you have to do is to go out there and show them that you are."

He'd actually come. There were so many things she wanted to say, but her throat was suddenly tight, and she couldn't force them out. "Hello," she said inadequately. "I'm glad you're here."

"I didn't have any choice." His lips were twitching. "I figured you'd be in a hell of a fix tonight without 'the ice beneath your skates.'"

She made a face. "Oh, dear, did I really say that? How hokey."

"Perhaps a little grandiloquent," he conceded, his eyes twinkling. "But I liked it all the same."

"That's good," she said softly. She was vaguely conscious Beau had drawn a few paces away in an attempt to give them a little privacy. A totally futile attempt, surrounded by people as they were. "I hope you were equally impressed by the rest of what I said."

"Very impressed, but you left before you let me answer the question you asked." He paused. "Yes."

"Yes?" she echoed bemusedly. "What question?"

He glanced impatiently around the crowded corridor before he said clearly, "Yes, I will marry you. Tonight if possible, tomorrow at the latest."

"Oh!" She smiled at him with heart-stopping brilliance. "Thank you."

There was a little flurry of laughter from those in the crowd who had been trying politely to pretend they weren't paying attention.

"You're very welcome," Anthony said gravely. "It's only the accepted thing to do with the lady who's the wind beneath your wings." He took a step closer and slowly drew one hand out of his coat pocket. He held it out to her, palm-upward. "A lady whom you love . . . and need."

It was too much. A gift so beautiful and touching, it filled every particle of her heart and soul with warmth and radiance. She put her hand in his. "Anthony, that's—"

"Come on, sugar," Beau said gently. "You've got to get ready. They'll be starting your music any second."

"What?" she asked dreamily. Then she came abruptly to attention. She gave Anthony's hand a quick squeeze and released it. "I'll be right back," she promised. "Wait for me."

He nodded. "I'll wait for you." His lips curved in a slight smile. "What's a few minutes more after fourteen years?"

Beau's hand was on her elbow urging her forward toward the ice. She could see the packed tiers of spectators now and hear the rustle of conversation from the stands as they caught sight of her. Beau held her steady as she removed her skate guards, his gaze fastened on her face. "Ready?"

She nodded serenely. "Ready."

She stepped onto the ice and skated to the center of the rink, scarcely hearing the burst of applause from the audience. She stood there alone, her head bent almost contemplatively while she waited for her music to begin. Ready? Yes, she was ready. After years of work, of tension, of disappointment, and of triumph, she was ready for this moment. How could she have been frightened when it was what she was meant to do? Dany wondered. All the ribbons of memory the past had woven told her that. Her music began. She raised her head, and there was such a look of luminous exultation on her face that there was a surprised murmur from the audience. She began to skate.

The long program had been choreographed as a complete change of pace from the short. The mood was to be lushly romantic and dreamlike. The haunting beauty of "Somewhere in Time" would merge with Rachmaninoff's *Rhapsody on a Theme of Paganini* for a triumphant crescendo, then drift gently back into the original theme for a touching and infinitely moving ending. She'd done the routine hundreds of times, but suddenly it was as if it were brand new. As if the world were brand new.

She felt lighter than morning air as she performed the first slow, exquisitely graceful movements. And the music! Oh, the music was part of her and she was part of the music. It beckoned to her and beguiled her and completed her. The poignantly beautiful Rachmaninoff theme was coming in now, and the mood changed to heart-lifting exultation. A split soaring for the sky, a triple, a layback spin reaching for the stars. Another triple. It was all so thrilling to know she was the shining center of that lovely music. Yet when the soft richness of the first theme began its encore, it was also absolutely right. Poetry, nostalgia, and a rapture that was all the more moving for the touch of sadness that lay beneath the free joyousness.

The audience was silent for a long emotion-charged moment as the program ended with Dany on her knees, her back arched, her arms rising above her head, and her face lifted with that same expression of radiant elation that had bewitched them in the first instant. The applause began, hesitant at first as if the audience were reluctant to wake from the spell she'd woven about them. Then it became a roaring, hysterical cacophony and swept roughly over her, jarring her out of her own dream.

She'd done it! No matter what the judges said, she'd never skated better in her entire life. She was on her feet, skating back to where Anthony was waiting, gathering flowers from the ice as she went. She waved and smiled, but she was scarcely aware of what she was doing. Her gaze was on the three people waiting for her just ahead. Anthony, Beau, and Marta. Her lover, her friends, her family.

Then Beau was enfolding her in a bear hug and whirling her around in an exuberant circle. There were tears pouring down Marta's cheeks as she grabbed Dany's shoulders the minute Beau put her down and shook her with the affectionate roughness of a lioness for her cub. "I told you you didn't have any competition," she said shakily. "I told you!" Someone was thrusting a huge bouquet of red roses into her arms and there were people all around her. But where was Anthony?

She drew a deep breath of relief as she saw him just on the outside of the perimeter of the crowd that was surrounding her. Dammit, he was doing it again, she thought with loving exasperation. Standing on the outside looking in. Letting her have all the triumph and adulation, making sure that both the victory and the spoils were entirely her own.

"Excuse me," she said, thrusting the bouquet at Marta. "Excuse me, I have to get through." The crowd was parting before her and then she was standing in front of Anthony.

"Hi," she said softly, stretching her hands out to him. "Thanks for waiting."

His silver-green eyes were suspiciously bright. "My pleasure," he said huskily, taking her hands in his. "How do you feel?"

She thought about it. "Proud, happy, eager for what's to come. How do you feel?"

His hands tightened on hers. "Proud. So proud. You were magic out there." His gaze went over her shoulder. "The technical scores are coming up. Don't you want to turn around and look at them?"

She shook her head. "No, I want to look at you." She wanted to remember always that expression of pride and love on his face. "You tell me what they are."

He read them off slowly as they flickered on. "All five point nine except for East Germany. He gave you a five eight." His eyes met hers worriedly. "It's going to be very close, Dany. We may not make it."

We. He hadn't wanted to steal even a little of her victory, but he would share her possible defeat. She felt a heady surge of pure love. "We may not," she agreed, smiling tranquilly. "But not because we didn't give it our best shot."

His eyes were on the scoreboard again, and she could feel the tension in him. "They're coming up." He began to read off the scores, but suddenly she couldn't hear him as the audience went wild. "Six, five point nine, six, six." His hands were tightening on hers with bone-crushing strength. "My God, even that bastard from East Germany gave you a five nine!"

"Is it enough?"

"You're damn right it's enough," he said thickly. "You've got it, Dany."

She had it. The gold. It was almost unbelievable. The noise was deafening, and the excitement surrounding her was nearly alive. But she was aware only of Anthony's hands holding hers, his eyes wrapping her in all the love and tenderness she could ever want.

She shook her head. "*We've* got it!" she corrected softly. "We, togetherness, the wind beneath *our* wings."

He smiled gently and then nodded slowly. "The wind beneath our wings."